# Grace Harlowe's Overland Riders Among the Kentucky Mountaineers

### Jessie Graham Flower

# Contents

CHAPTER I EXCITEMENT IN THE FOOTHILLS ..................................................7

CHAPTER II THE MYSTERY MAN ....................................................................15

CHAPTER III HIPPY BOUNCES THE "SHEREEF"...........................................19

CHAPTER IV FOOTPRINTS IN THE MOSS ......................................................25

CHAPTER V THE WAY IS BARRED ..................................................................31

CHAPTER VI HIPPY MYSTERIOUSLY DISAPPEARS .....................................36

CHAPTER VII A VOICE FROM THE SHADOWS................................................43

CHAPTER VIII A FRIEND IN NEED ..................................................................50

CHAPTER IX THE POWER OF MIND ................................................................57

CHAPTER X "THEY'VE GOT THE BOY".............................................................62

CHAPTER XI "A MARKED MAN" .......................................................................66

CHAPTER XII A MOUNTAIN MYSTERY ...........................................................70

CHAPTER XIII THREE MEN IN THE CORNFIELD............................................77

CHAPTER XIV ELFREDA DISTINGUISHES HERSELF ....................................82

CHAPTER XV WHEN EMMA SAID TOO MUCH ..............................................87

CHAPTER XVI A JOKE ON THE OVERLANDERS .............................................95

CHAPTER XVII THE DANCE AT COON HOLLOW ...........................................99

CHAPTER XVIII AN INTERRUPTED PARTY ...................................................106

CHAPTER XIX A CALL FOR HELP ..................................................................112

CHAPTER XX HIPPY AS A ROUGHRIDER .....................................................118

CHAPTER XXI AN APOLOGY AND A THREAT................................................124

CHAPTER XXII JULIE BRINGS DISTURBING NEWS .....................................128

CHAPTER XXIII THE GATHERING OF THE CLANS .......................................135

CHAPTER XXIV TRAIL'S END .........................................................................145

# GRACE HARLOWE'S OVERLAND RIDERS AMONG THE KENTUCKY MOUNTAINEERS

BY

Jessie Graham Flower

# CHAPTER I
## EXCITEMENT IN THE FOOTHILLS

The foothills of the Kentucky Mountains echoed to the strains of a rollicking college song, as Grace Harlowe's Overland Riders rode into a laurel-bordered clearing and dismounted to make their first camp of this, their third summer's outing in the saddle.

Only one of the party remained on his mount. This one was Washington Washington, the colored boy that they had taken on at Henderson to be their man of all work, guide and assistant cook, for Washington had declared that, "Ah knows more 'bout de mountings dan any oder niggah in Kaintuck." On his own recommendation, Grace and her party had accepted him.

Washington, however, already had shown a love of leisure that was not wholly in keeping with his further recommendation for activity, and, instead of assisting the girls of the Overland unit to unload their ponies, the boy sat perched on the pack mule that he had been riding, playing a harmonica, swaying in his saddle in rhythm with the music, and rolling the whites of his eyes in ecstasy.

"Just look at him, girls," urged Grace Harlowe Gray laughingly. "If that isn't a picture!"

"I call it a nightmare," objected Emma Dean. "Oh, if I only had a nice ripe tomato, and could throw straight enough."

"Impossible!" declared Elfreda Briggs, whereupon Anne Nesbit and Nora Wingate broke forth into merry peals of laughter.

"Laundry!" roared Hippy Wingate. "We didn't hire you for a moving picture. Shake your lazy bones and get busy. If you don't hustle you'll get something harder than a tomato."

"Laundry?" wondered Tom Gray. "Why Laundry, Hippy?"

"That's his name, isn't it? Doesn't he call himself Washington Washington on Sundays and holidays, and Wash-Wash, for short, on weekdays? I have his word for it. Wash is laundry and laundry is wash in the neck of the woods where I was reared," explained Hippy, at the same time narrowly observing the colored boy, who, following Lieutenant Wingate's threat, had permitted himself to slide to the ground, and there he sat, still mouthing his harmonica, lost to everything but the music he was creating.

"Your logic is unassailable," nodded Miss Briggs. "I was wondering why, while we are about it, we don't hire a brass band. We at least would not be obliged to listen to the same tune all the time. Does any one know of a way to put a mute on a harmonica?"

"Ah reckon Ah do," mimicked Emma Dean, taking careful aim and shying a pebble at Wash.

The pebble went rather wide of the mark--that is, the mark for which it was intended, but it reached another and a fully as satisfactory one. The pebble hit Washington's pack mule on the tender part of its hind leg, galvanizing that member into instant and vigorous action.

The eyes of the Overlanders were not quick enough to see the movement that followed. What they did see, however, was Washington Washington lifted from the ground and pitched head first into a clump of laurel, where the light foot of an outraged mule had landed him.

"He's killed!" cried Anne, voicing the thought that was in the mind of each of her companions, and a concerted rush was made for the clump of laurel.

They found the colored boy somewhat dazed when they dragged him from the bushes.

"Wha--whar dat 'monica?" he gasped, referring to the harmonica that he was playing when the mule kicked him.

"Maybe he swallowed it," suggested Emma. "I hope not, for he surely would have musical indigestion. Wouldn't that be terrible--for us?"

"No great loss if it has landed over in the Cumberlands," observed Tom Gray. "Wash, where did the mule hit you?"

"Ah reckons all ovah, 'cept on de bean. Why dat fool mule kick me? Hain't ne-vah done nothin' laik that befo'. Ah ask yuh why he do dat?" insisted Washington.

They glanced at Emma, whose face reddened.

"I threw a stone at you and hit the mule, if you must know," she said. "The mule passed it on, hitting you with his foot. That mule must have played tag when he was a child. I'm sorry, Wash--but if you had been attending to your business you would not have been hit."

Washington's first thought upon recovering from his daze had been for the harmonica, and his first act, after getting to his feet, was to go in search of it. He found it after considerable effort, and ran the scales on it.

"Glory be!" cried the boy. "Dat fool mule ain't done kicked de music out ob it."

"Listen to me, Washington," demanded Grace, stepping over and laying a firm hand on the lad's shoulder. "You will put that instrument away--"

"'Tain't no inst'ment. Hit's a 'monica," he interrupted.

"I am speaking. Put it away, and do not let me see you touch it again until you have finished your work. Do you understand?"

"Uh-huh."

"See that you do not forget. Unpack both mule packs, but look out for the mules' heels, and remember that we did not hire you for an ornament. Emma Dean, let this be a warning to you," admonished Grace, turning to her companion. "Never trifle with a mule. They are all notoriously devoid of a sense of humor."

Washington, in the meantime, had shuffled away and had leisurely begun removing the packs.

"Speaking of ornaments, I suppose I am the only real ornament in this outfit," observed Hippy.

"You mean the kind that they pack away in the garret with broken chairs and old chromos," suggested Emma.

Hippy shrugged his shoulders and walked away, followed by the laughter of his companions. Emma had scored again, as she frequently did, and Hippy, instead of being ruffled, took keen delight, as usual, in her repartee.

"I fear that boy is not going to do at all," said Grace's husband with a shake of the head. "As I have remarked before, you should have a man for a guide, a man who knows these mountains and who is able to protect and look out for you girls in the event of your getting into trouble."

"But, Tom dear, don't you think the Overland girls by this time should be quite able to look out for themselves?" begged Grace.

"Ordinarily, yes. You are, however, going into territory that is rather wild, going among people that do not value human life or liberty according to our standards. My friend, Colonel Spotsworth, of Louisville, strongly advised against you folks crossing the eastern end of the range, which would take you through mountains where moonshiners and feudists hold forth. I agree with him."

"We have Hippy," suggested Elfreda. "In an emergency he is worth half a dozen of the ordinary kind."

"Yes, but Hippy is not a woodsman. He knows nothing at all about woodcraft, a necessary accomplishment in one who is going to pilot a party of girls across such mountain territory as you propose to travel."

"What's that you say, Tom Gray?" called Lieutenant Wingate from the campfire where he was observing Washington fan it into life.

Grace laughingly repeated what Tom had said.

"Humph! I know all I need to know about woodcraft," declared Hippy with emphasis. "When I smell wood burning in the kitchen stove I know it is time to eat. What more knowledge of woodcraft does a fellow need?"

"Amply sufficient for you, Hippy. But what about the rest of the party?" grinned Tom Gray.

"As I was about to say," resumed Grace, "we shall be up with you in a few weeks. How long do you reckon it will take you to finish your government contract to survey that tract in the Cumberlands?"

"Possibly four weeks. Not longer."

"Call it three weeks--three weeks from to-day. That will make it the twenty-fifth. We will try to be in the vicinity of Hall's Corners on that date, and if you are not there we will wait for you. You will do the same provided we are late in reaching the Corners. Let's have a look at the contour map," suggested Grace.

While the others of the party were busy setting the camp to rights, Washington having removed the packs from the mules, Grace and Tom pored over the map of the eastern section of the mountains. Not only were they planning their routes, but they were critically examining a portion of the map that was encircled with a ring of red ink. The space within the circle represented a tract of mountain land that belonged to Lieutenant Hippy Wingate, property that he had inherited.

Hippy had never seen this property, it having been left to him by a wealthy uncle whose large fortune Hippy had inherited while fighting the Germans in the air in France. He now proposed to look it over. In fact, this journey of the Overland Riders had been planned with that object in view.

Following their return from France, where they had served in the Overton College Unit, Grace having been an ambulance driver at the front, the girls had decided to seek recreation in the saddle each summer. Their first vacation was spent in an exciting ride over the Old Apache Trail in Arizona, following this with a venturesome journey on horseback across the arid waste of the Great American Desert. Lieutenant Wingate's determination to visit his property in the Kentucky Mountains led the Overland Riders, as Grace Harlowe and her friends called themselves, to make those mountains the objective of their third vacation in the saddle.

After Tom Gray had finished his government survey, it was their purpose to proceed with him to Lieutenant Wingate's tract, where Tom was to make a survey and examination of it, so that Hippy might learn whether or not the property possessed any particular value.

"Hippy says his uncle took the property in payment of a debt, but that the uncle never had considered it to be worth much of anything," said Tom reflectively. "From what little I know of that section of the country, I am inclined to agree with him. However, we shall see when we get there."

"Who knows but that Hippy may find still another fortune awaiting him there?" suggested Grace.

Tom shook his head and smiled.

"It would be Hippy's luck, wouldn't it? He doesn't need it; he already has more money than he knows what to do with. Nor have I the slightest hope that he will find anything of value there. The twenty-fifth, then, it is. I shall make Chapman's my base and work from there. If necessary to communicate with me in the meantime you may address me there. I--"

"What's this? Henpecking your husband again, Grace Harlowe?" teased Hippy, coming up to them at this juncture.

"Yes, Hip. I am a shining example of a much henpecked husband. What would you do were you a henpecked husband?" questioned Tom quizzically. "Come, now!"

"Well," reflected Hippy, "I think that would depend largely upon the hen."

"You are right," agreed Tom Gray laughingly. "I shall be leaving in the morning, old man, and I have agreed with Grace to meet the Overland outfit at Hall's Corners three weeks from to-day, or as near to that date as possible. We will then make a pilgrimage to the lands of one Lieutenant Wingate and see what we shall find there. Probably nothing more than some wild game, a few rattlers and--and some mountaineers," added Tom significantly.

"I have been thinking, Tom and Grace, that, should we discover anything of real value there, the Overland Riders should share in it. This is a sort of exploration party, and to the discoverers should belong the spoils," declared Hippy.

Tom shook his head.

"No, no," protested Grace. "It is fine of you to make the offer, but I could not permit it for myself, and I am positive that the other girls will not even listen to it."

"You see, Tom, how they spurn me. The instant I get a brilliant thought they promptly duck it in ice water," complained Hippy.

"We will do this much, we will be your guests when we reach your domains, and, if you insist on being liberal, you may cook our meals for us three times a day. However, so far as sharing in your good fortune is concerned, we can do so only in our hearts," decided Grace with emphasis.

Grace immediately acquainted her companions with Hippy's unselfish offer to share with them whatever good fortune might be in store for him in the Kentucky Mountains.

"That is splendid of Hippy," declared Anne, smiling and nodding.

"I tell him, however, that when we are his guests in the Hippy Mountains, he can give us three good meals a day, cooked by his own fair hands, but that is all," announced Grace. "Do I echo your sentiments, girls?"

They said she did. That is, all except Emma Dean agreed with Grace Harlowe. Emma warned them that Hippy had better not offer her a share in anything unless he were prepared in his heart to lose it.

"Very good then, I won't. I withdraw the offer," declared Hippy airily. "I will agree to cook a meal for you over on the range. Mark the words, 'cook a meal for you on the range!' Ha-ha. How is that? I reckon I can stand it to cook a meal for you if you can stand it to eat it. Speaking of food reminds me that I smell bacon frying, so suppose we fall to and devour it, provided it is fit to eat. Personally I am not overloaded with confidence in Laundry's ability as a chef."

Night had settled over the mountains when they finally sat down on the ground by the campfire to eat their supper, the first warm meal they had had since starting out on their journey at daylight that morning.

Washington had done very well with his first meal, considering that he so recently had been kicked out of camp by an irate mule, and the Overland girls admitted that the little colored boy did know how to cook after all, for the bacon, the coffee, and the potatoes, baked in their jackets in hot ashes, were delicious.

The girls, however, had already found it necessary to read Wash a lecture on the beauties of neatness and cleanliness, it having been discovered that, in this direction, Wash-Wash was not all that his nickname implied.

Wash, having been given permission, retired to the edge of the laurel to resume his harmonica exercise. Lying back in the shadows, only the whites of his eyes and the reflection of the light from the campfire on teeth and harmonica were visible to the Overlanders, giving merely a suggestion of a human countenance.

"A nature sketch in black and white," observed Anne Nesbit. "I should think he would weary of blowing that thing so much. He has been doing so all day long."

"Blowing? You are wrong," corrected Hippy. "A harmonica is played with a grunt and a sigh. I could make a brand new pun on that if I wanted to, but--"

"Don't you dare," begged Miss Briggs. "I am long-suffering, but I cannot tolerate the ancient quality of your puns."

"Most spinsters are that way," retorted Lieutenant Wingate. "Tom, have you any orders for me? I suppose I shall have to act as guardian for your wife while you are absent from this outfit. If you have half as difficult a time managing her as I do, I don't envy you your lot. The only bright spot in the situation is that I have to put up with her peculiarities for the duration of this journey only. You are in for life."

"Hippy, I am ashamed of you," rebuked Nora Wingate.

"Thank you. You see, Tom, what a helpmate my little Nora is. I don't have to feel ashamed of any act of mine; I don't have to feel embarrassed after I have put my foot in it, nor anything. Nora does all of that for me. Really, Tom, you ought to train

Grace to be ashamed for you for your shortcomings, or to be embarrassed for you. You have no idea what a lot of bother over nothing it relieves a fellow of."

"Nora Wingate is a very busy woman," observed Emma, whereat there was a laugh at Hippy's expense.

"Tom Gray's wife doesn't have to apologize for him," laughed Grace. "Folks, don't you think this conversation is growing rather personal? I would suggest that we all put on the brakes and start something less personal."

The brakes were instantly put on in one direction, but wholly released in another. The music from Washington's harmonica ceased suddenly in the midst of a lofty flight, ending in a gurgle and a gasp. The Overlanders heard it and laughed.

"He's swallowed the music box!" cried Emma.

Wash, finding his voice, uttered a shrill scream of fright that brought the Overland Riders to their feet in alarm. They were amazed to see the colored boy charging across the camp, his feet barely touching the ground, his eyes wide and staring. In his flight he bowled over Grace Harlowe who measured her length on the ground on her back.

"Stop!" shouted Tom Gray, making a grab for the boy, and missing him by an inch or so.

Emma Dean stuck out a foot and succeeded better than she had hoped, for Washington tripped and plunged floundering into the campfire.

Uttering a piercing yell, he bounded up like a rubber ball and made a mad dash for the bushes with Hippy Wingate in full pursuit.

# CHAPTER II
# THE MYSTERY MAN

I've got him," cried Hippy, appearing with a firm grip on the frightened Washington's arm, and fairly dragging him along. "Can't afford to let any fellow get away who can bake potatoes like Wash can."

"Bring him to me, please," demanded Grace. "Now, Washington, what happened to frighten you so?" she asked in a soothing tone, at the same time patting the colored boy on his kinky head.

Wash rolled his eyes from side to side and twisted his head as if to smooth out the wrinkles in his neck muscles.

"Speak up. Don't be afraid. Nothing can harm you. What was it?" urged Grace.

"De--de debbil him--him speak--him heyeh. Him speak to Wash right outer de air," gasped the boy.

"There! I knew something terrible would happen from your awful work on that harmonica," declared Emma Dean. "I'm not at all surprised, Wash."

Grace shook her head at Emma.

"You imagined all of that, Wash," she said. "What did you think you heard him say?"

"Him say--right outer de air, 'Wash! Remembah, dis am de sebbenth yeah.' Den Ah tuk a frenzy spell."

"What do you mean by the seventh year?" questioned Miss Briggs.

"Ah doan know. It's de hoodoo, Miss. Somet'n sure gwine happen to dis niggah."

"Nonsense!" retorted Nora sharply.

"If you don't brace up and behave yourself, something surely will happen to you," warned Lieutenant Wingate.

"I believe the boy really did hear something," declared Grace as she gazed at the trembling lad before her. "Tom, please look there where he was sitting, will you?"

Tom Gray rose and started to obey her request. At this juncture the bushes parted, and a man, faintly outlined in the light from the campfire, stepped into view.

Wash saw him and, uttering another yell, made a break, but Hippy, on the watch for this very thing, caught and held him.

"Behave yourself or I'll let the fellow have you," he warned.

Tom hesitated, then stepped forward to meet the stranger. He saw a man apparently of early middle age, smooth-shaven, wearing long iron-gray hair that hung below his sombrero, the locks curling slightly at the bottom. The eyes that regarded Tom were keen and twinkling, full of good nature and humor.

"Well, sir, who are you?" demanded Grace's husband.

"Who am I? You will be surprised when I tell you. I'm the original Mystery Man. Spectacles, notions and trinkets are my specialty. I make the near blind see and dull the glare of the sun for those who do see."

"Glad to meet you. Come in, won't you?" invited Tom.

"That's what I'm here for. I've invited myself to have a snack with you-all."

Grace said they had just eaten, but that they would prepare something for their caller if he could wait. The stranger said he could and would wait, so Anne and Nora set about making coffee and frying bacon, Washington being still in too great a fright to do anything useful.

"I'll introduce myself again," resumed the caller. "I'm Jeremiah Long, and that's the long and short of it. Who are you?"

Grace introduced the members of her party, telling Long that they were riding for their health and amusement. Emma added that they were on their way in search of a fortune on Lieutenant Wingate's tract of mountain land, and would have said more had not Grace given her a warning look.

"Are you the voice from the wilderness?" demanded Hippy scowlingly.

The stranger threw back his head and laughed.

"I confess it. I am the 'seventh year' man. Couldn't resist the temptation to give the pickaninny a scare. Oh, thank you," he added as Nora handed a heaping plate of food to him and a tin cup full of steaming coffee.

"You are a peddler. Is that it?" questioned Emma.

"Heavens, no! I'm a promoter. I promote the well-being of these good mountain folks by giving them sight and by furnishing them with nick-nacks to delight the eye. If you-all are troubled with poor sight I'll be happy to fit you with glasses warranted to make you see double. More coffee, if you please. This is the real article. I think I'll have to make this camp my headquarters."

"This camp will be some miles from here by this time to-morrow," Grace Harlowe informed him.

"So will I. So will I. No bother at all about that. Wash, come here!"

Washington would not budge, so Hippy led him over to the caller.

"Scared you, didn't I, eh? Mebby it is the seventh year, but don't let that bother you. Here! Here's a new harmonica for you. It will make more noise than the one you lost when I whispered in your ear out yonder. Go on now, and behave yourself," he added, giving Wash a playful push. "What can I do for you, folks?"

"I suppose you know this country well?" questioned Grace.

Long shrugged his shoulders.

"Sometimes I think I do, then I discover that I don't," he replied soberly. "No one knows it. I know the people, on the surface, and know my way around."

"Perhaps you know something about the moonshiners and the feudists?" suggested Nora.

Jeremiah Long gave her a quick glance of inquiry.

"Take a word of advice from the Mystery Man. The less you know about anything up here in these hills the better off you are in the end. Some folks have made the mistake of knowing too much for their own good, and some of them are here yet, but they ain't saying anything."

Grace thanked him and agreed that his advice was good, at the same time speculating in her own mind over their guest. She was not wholly satisfied that he was what he pretended to be, but what he was in reality, she could not even guess.

In the meantime, Washington, lost in admiration of his new possession, was drawing harmony, and some discord, from it and rolling his eyes soulfully. In the ecstasy of the moment he had forgotten his recent fright. Tom and the Mystery

Man were engaged in conversation, Hippy now and then interjecting a question, for the topic under discussion was the tract of land owned by Hippy, though not since Emma's remark had any reference been made to Hippy's ownership of it. The guest's talk was largely about the lay of the land there and its possibilities.

"I'll see you folks if you are going there," he promised finally. "I shall be in that section of the range about three weeks from now, and maybe I can do you some good."

"Thank you," smiled Grace. "We shall be pleased to see you then or at any other time. Mr. Gray leaves to-morrow morning for the Cumberlands where he has business, and we hope to join him, or rather to have him join us, in about that time. I think--"

"Hulloa the camp!" shouted a voice from the bushes on the opposite side of the camp from that by which Mr. Long had entered.

"Hulloa yourself!" bellowed Hippy Wingate. "Come in. The door's wide open."

An instant later a man stepped into the camp, a rifle slung under one arm, a revolver hanging from his belt in its holster. He was tall, gaunt and raw-boned, a typical Kentucky mountaineer, and, as he stood there surveying the Overland Riders from beneath his broad-brimmed hat, not a word was spoken on either side. The mountaineer was studying the members of the Overland party, and the Overland Riders were regarding him inquiringly.

"Why, where is--" began Emma Dean, but a gesture from Grace checked her. Not so with Washington Washington, however.

"Whar dat man?" he cried, referring to their first visitor.

A quick glance about the camp revealed to the amazed Overlanders that Jeremiah Long, the Mystery Man, had suddenly and mysteriously disappeared. No one had seen or heard him go. He had simply melted away.

## CHAPTER III
## HIPPY BOUNCES THE "SHEREEF"

Still the newcomer stood peering into the faces of the Overlanders. Hippy began talking to the man with his fingers in the deaf and dumb system. The stranger regarded him frowningly, then shifted his rifle into his right hand. "Who be yuh?" demanded the man.

"Oh! I thought you were a dummy," apologized Hippy. "A thousand pardons, old man."

"May I ask who *you* are and what you wish?" questioned Grace pleasantly, as she stepped forward.

"Ah asked yuh first. Who be yuh?"

"We are a party from the north, riding through the Kentucky Mountains partly for pleasure, partly for business reasons."

"Whut business?"

"That is a personal question, is it not?" smiled Grace. "Won't you sit down and rest before you go on? We shall be glad to have you do so."

"Be yuh goin' to answer mah question?"

"I think not, sir."

"Ah'll tell yuh who Ah be, then, an' mebby yuh'll answer. Ah'm the dep'y Shereef of this 'ere deestric'. Ah kin land yuh all in the calaboose if Ah wants to."

"Deputy Sheriff! Mercy to goodness!" murmured Emma. "Next thing we know, the Lord High Executioner will be calling on us looking for victims to decapitate."

"Yes?" questioned Grace.

"Let me speak with the man," urged Tom Gray, whereupon Grace waved her hand behind her to warn Tom to keep quiet.

"Who be yuh?"

"Presumably the man means to ask 'Who are you?' but unfortunately he doesn't speak English," said Emma in a voice loud enough for the mountaineer to hear. He glared at her and Emma glared back.

"I think, sir," replied Grace Harlowe, "that this has gone far enough. We have no information to give. I am sorry, sir. Our purpose in visiting these mountains is a proper one. We are violating no law, have committed no crime, and therefore can have no interest for a deputy sheriff. Besides, I do not believe you are a deputy sheriff!"

The stranger shifted uneasily. Hippy had risen and was stretching himself and yawning.

"All Ah've got to say is, yuh-all git out o' these mountings right smart or Ah'll take yuh-all in. T'morrow mornin' yuh git!"

"Thank you." Grace smiled sweetly.

Hippy strolled up to the mountaineer, also smiling, with right hand extended as if about to shake hands with their caller, but as he neared the man the smile suddenly left his face, and he inhaled a long full breath.

"Beat it!" exploded Lieutenant Wingate in the mountaineer's ear, at the same time turning the man about and running him out of camp in bouncer fashion.

"Run, Mr. Man! Run as if the Old Harry were after you, and don't forget to keep that rifle pointed away from the camp. If it goes off you're liable to get hurt. Get out!"

The mountaineer, as Hippy released him, sprang away a few paces, then, suddenly whirling, fired point blank at Hippy.

Expecting this very move, Lieutenant Wingate had dropped down the instant he saw the man turning, and the bullet went over Hippy's head, and incidentally over the heads of the Overland Riders in the camp a few yards to the rear.

Lieutenant Wingate was unarmed, his revolver being in its holster on his saddle, so all he could do was to duck. His experience as a fighting aviator in France had made Hippy somewhat callous to bullets, as well as an expert in ducking. In the present instance, Lieutenant Wingate made so many ducks and dives, side-slips and Immelman turns that the mountaineer, crack shot that he was, found himself unable to score a hit. The darkness, too, prevented his getting a good sight at the man he was trying to shoot.

Back in the camp the rest of the Overland outfit were lying flat on the ground, just as they used to do in France when they heard a shell coming, which might be due to land somewhere near them. Not one of them had a weapon handy, nor would they have dared use them had weapons been at hand, because there was no telling where Hippy Wingate was at any given second. That, too, was what was troubling the mountaineer.

At the first shot, Washington Washington had forsaken the harmonica and dived head first into the bushes where he lay, face down, a finger stuck in either ear.

Hippy's floundering finally ceased and the mountaineer could not find him. Believing, perhaps, that he had hit his victim, the fellow began shooting into the camp of the Overlanders.

"I'm not going to lie here and let that fellow kill us all," declared Grace Harlowe, springing up and starting away on a zigzagging run. "Keep down, all of you. I'll fetch weapons," she called back.

Tom Gray, however, had forestalled her, and, leaping to his feet, had run back to the tethering ground, where the ponies and their equipment had been placed for the night, to fetch rifles.

Tom and Grace were back in a few moments, but instead of stepping out into the open space where the tents were pitched and the campfire was burning, they separated and crept around opposite sides of the camp, over which bullets continued to whistle at intervals.

"That you, Grace?" demanded a cautious voice a few yards to her right.

"Hippy! Are you wounded?" begged Grace.

"I *am* not. I'm trying to get to my rifle."

"Here. Take mine. Look out for Tom. He is on the opposite side of the camp. We agreed not to go beyond the edge of the clearing so there might be no danger of our hitting each other. He is looking for the 'shereef.'"

"I'll fix him. Hark! Did you hear that?"

"Yes. It was a revolver shot on beyond where Tom is," answered Grace.

"There it goes again. Tom must be using his revolver. A hit! Somebody yelled," cried Lieutenant Wingate. "I hope it is that pesky mosquito that has been trying to sting us. Stay here while I go out to investigate."

"No, no!" protested Grace. "If you do you and Tom surely will shoot at each other. Remember he is a woodsman and knows how to creep up on one without making a sound that a human being could hear half a dozen yards away. Go to the edge of the clearing and wait. I will go back and around on Tom's side of the camp."

Grace crept away, calling softly to the girls to keep down. Washington, with his ears muffled, failed to hear her coming, nor had she given the little colored boy a thought until she planked a foot down on his neck.

Wash uttered a yell and leaped to his feet, for the second time that night bowling Grace over and darting deeper into the bush.

"Oh, that impossible boy!" complained Grace. "He nearly frightened me out of my wits. The firing has stopped. I must know what has happened."

Grace crept on cautiously, listening intently, not knowing what moment she might come upon the mountaineer. Either he had been hit or he was still stalking the camp, and she must settle the question in her mind before she would feel safe to settle down for the night.

"Is that you, Grace?" demanded a low, guarded voice just ahead of her.

"Oh, yes! Gracious, Tom, you gave me a start that time! Where is the man?"

"Gone away."

"Was it you who shot at him?"

"No. I was just about to let him have it when some one fired two shots from a revolver. The second shot hit the man in his shoulder, I think, spinning him clean around and dropping him. He was up and staggering away in a few seconds. I followed him for some little distance; then, being satisfied that he was trying to get away, I came back."

"I hope he stays away," said Grace with emphasis.

"He may be back in force," answered Tom. "I could easily have hit the fellow, and was about to put a bullet through his leg when the revolver shots were fired. Say, Grace! You did not do that, did you?"

"No, Tom, I did not, nor do I know who did. Let's go into camp."

They got up and walked briskly back, calling out to the Overlanders that they were coming.

"He has gone," cried Grace as the two emerged into the clearing.

"Tom, did you wing the critter?" demanded Hippy.

"Hippy, did you fire those shots?" demanded Tom Gray, each asking his question at the same time.

There was a laugh from the girls, and another laugh when both men replied in chorus, "I did not!"

"Where's Washington?" asked Miss Briggs.

"I heard him yell," answered Hippy. "Hope the kid hasn't gotten into trouble. I'll go look for him."

"Yes," spoke up Grace. "I stepped on his neck and he uttered a frightful howl and ran away."

"The question now appears to be, 'Who killed Cock Robin?'" observed Emma Dean. "We know who stepped on Laundry's neck, but we do not know who fired the fatal shot."

"Mystery, mystery, mystery!" complained Miss Briggs. "This is only our first day out and we have involved ourselves in a maze of it, with an excellent foundation laid for future trouble."

"All because that husband of mine ran that deputy sheriff out of our camp," wailed Nora. "Hippy will be the death of all of us yet."

"Hippy did exactly right," approved Tom Gray. "What I am thinking about now is why the mountaineer came here to order us out. I have my suspicions, and I don't like the outlook at all."

"Don't worry, Tom dear," soothed Grace.

"Yes, the worst is yet to come," called Hippy Wingate, at this juncture appearing leading Washington Washington by the ear. "I found Laundry hiding in the bushes. Sit down there and behave yourself, Little Snowdrop, and let that harmonica alone for the rest of the night. Will some one tell me what became of Jeremiah Long?"

"The Mystery Man is here," announced a voice, and the spectacle man walked up rubbing his hands and smiling in great good humor. "What's the excitement?"

"Where did you go so suddenly?" demanded Hippy frowningly.

"I went out to stake down my horse and get my store--my grip. Did I not hear shooting?"

"Yes. We had a visitor and--" Emma bubbled over with words as she described what had occurred after Long's departure, to all of which he listened attentively.

"Somebody, we don't know who, shot him in the shoulder. Who do you think could have done that, Mr. Long?"

"Very mysterious, very mysterious," answered the Mystery Man.

Grace and Elfreda were regarding him keenly.

"Think I'll pitch my camp by your fire to-night, if you haven't any objection," announced the visitor.

"You are quite welcome," offered Tom. "If you wish to, you can bunk in with the lieutenant and myself. There is room for three in our tent. We could not think of letting you sleep outside in this chill air."

"Outside for me," answered Mr. Long. "Must have air and plenty of it. You see I heat it up inside of me and use it later to sell my goods. A promoter, you know, must depend upon hot air because what he's selling won't float on cold air."

Grace brought out blankets and a pneumatic pillow which she placed in a heap near the fire.

"Make up your bed on the softest spot you can find, Mr. Long, though I do not believe there is much choice," said Grace. Then, in a lower voice: "I hope you may not find it necessary to shoot any more mountaineers to-night, Mr. Long."

"Sh--h--h--h--h!" warned the Mystery Man. "I don't know what you're talking about," he added in a louder tone, observing that Washington Washington was standing close by, all eyes and ears.

Grace walked away laughing, Jeremiah Long observing her with twinkling eyes, a quizzical smile on his face.

# CHAPTER IV
# FOOTPRINTS IN THE MOSS

Tom Gray had planned to make an early start next morning, so he was up just before break of day, lighting the cook-fire that Washington had laid for him. Wisps of smoke from the fire were wafted into Grace's tent, awakening her instantly.

"Well, Tom, you thought you would steal a march on me, didn't you?" she chided, as she came out unbraiding her hair.

"I hoped I might. That was why I said good-bye last night."

"You did not think for a moment that I would let you go away without my getting up to see you off, did you?" she wondered. "No. You should have known better than that."

"Now that you are here, I will speak what is in my mind. Watch yourself, Grace. That affair last night disturbs me not a little, because it is an indication of what you folks may have to contend with up here. The Kentucky mountaineer is not a gentle animal. He is a man of almost primitive instincts, and the worst of him is that he doesn't come out in the open to settle a grudge, but, as a rule, settles it from ambush."

"You forget, Tom dear, that we girls are not tenderfeet, that we are seasoned veterans of the world war and that the whistle of a bullet is not a new nor a particularly terrifying sound to us. I hope you will not worry about us. In three weeks you will be with us. By the way, when did our Mystery Man leave?"

"When? Why--I--I didn't know--"

"You had not even discovered that he had gone?" chuckled Grace. "Oh, Tom! There are his blankets within a yard of you, neatly folded, and a slip of paper pinned to the top one, probably bidding us good-bye and thanking us for our hospitality.

Read it, please."

Tom did so and nodded.

"Just what you thought it was, Grace. You must be gifted with second sight. About the man Jeremiah Long, who calls himself the Mystery Man, I have a thought that he is the fellow who shot the mountaineer last night."

"Tom dear, you're really awake at last, and before breakfast, too. I am proud of you, my husband. Indeed I am," teased Grace.

"Don't laugh at me. I will confess that it never occurred to me until a few moments ago. There *is* something mysterious about the fellow, and I confess that I cannot make him out."

Grace nodded and her face took on a thoughtful expression.

"He is not only mysterious, but very keen. Last night--I don't know whether or not you noted the fact--he heard that mountaineer approaching, and slipped out of camp. I do not believe he went far, but that where he was he could see and hear all that was going on. Later he must have hurried around to the rear of the camp, and, when the fellow was trying to shoot Hippy, Long put a bullet through our caller's shoulder. I call that good shooting."

"Hm--m--m--m! Now that you speak of it, I do recall that he disappeared rather suddenly. I am grateful for what he did for us, of course, but, Grace, I do not wholly trust the man, and, if he comes again, I should watch him, were I in your place."

"I do not agree with you at all, Tom. The man is a mystery, but I am convinced that nothing bad lurks behind those twinkling eyes. However, we shall undoubtedly know more about him later, for I have a feeling that Jeremiah will play an important part in our operations up here in the Kentucky mountains. We won't get worked up over him at present, anyway. To change the subject, I haven't told you that Elfreda has adopted Little Lindy, the hermit's daughter that we took from the cave in the Specter Mountains last season. The Overlanders are still her guardians, but that guardianship will be transferred to Elfreda when we get back home in the fall."

"Lindy is a lucky girl. The silver mine is panning out big and she will be a very rich girl by the time she comes of age. Have a cup of coffee with me?"

"Yes, Tom."

While Tom was eating his breakfast, he and Grace discussed their personal affairs, then Grace walked with him to the tethering ground, first having seen to it that Tom's pack contained sufficient food to last him through his journey of several days to the Cumberlands. Good-byes were then said and Tom rode away.

After watering the ponies, Grace returned to camp and sat by the fire thinking, until it was time to call her companions. By the time they came out she had breakfast ready for them. Washington, who slept in a little pup-tent, had to be dragged out by the feet by Hippy before he was sufficiently awake to function.

"Laundry," said Hippy solemnly, "I hope you never get caught in a burning house in the night. If you are, the house and yourself will be a heap of ashes in the cellar by the time you get awake."

"Listen to him, will you, Nora Wingate," cackled Emma Dean hoarsely, for the chill of the mountain morning had gotten into her throat.

"For your information, Miss Dean, I will say that the only time my Nora ever listens to her husband is when he talks in his sleep." A pained expression appeared on Hippy's face when he said it.

"Go on wid ye," laughed Nora. "Ye know ye can't talk in your sleep because your snores don't give ye a chance."

Grace put an end to the argument by announcing that breakfast was served. The girls regarded Grace inquiringly when she informed them that their late guest, the Mystery Man, had again vanished with his usual mysteriousness.

"He hath folded his tent and stolen away," observed Emma Dean dramatically.

"He didn't fold his tent, for he hadn't any tent to fold," differed Hippy. "He folded his blankets and hiked for the tall timber. How far do we ride to-day, Grace?"

"To Spring Brook. Wash, how far from here is the next camping place?" questioned Grace, turning to the colored boy.

"Wall, Ah reckons it's 'bout er whoop an' er holler from heyeh."

"So far as that?" chuckled Hippy Wingate.

"It's terrible! I know I never shall be able to stand it to ride so far," declared Emma, tilting her nose up, her head inclined over her right shoulder, a characteristic pose for her when she thought she was saying something smart. As usual, her remark brought a laugh.

"Emma Dean, your nose is the last word in neat impertinence," declared Elfreda Briggs. "Were you a man, some one surely would flatten it for you. Forgive me, dear. That was rude of me," apologized J. Elfreda.

"Never mind the apology. I am used to being abused by my companions," retorted Emma, her face a little redder than usual.

Grace laughingly interrupted the badinage by directing Washington to begin packing. She said they must make an early start, not knowing how far it was to their day's destination, but which, she believed, from a perusal of her map, was all of twenty-five miles.

"The trails are no more than foot-paths and we can make no time, so let's go," she urged.

It was an hour later when the party mounted and started away, Washington bringing up the rear on a pack mule, industriously playing his new harmonica. The going was slow and tedious and the Overlanders were tired when they halted for a rest and luncheon shortly before noon. A half hour's nap followed the luncheon, the party being "lulled" to sleep by Washington's harmonica.

It was a discordant, insistent screeching of the harmonica that finally awakened them.

"Stop that noise!" roared Hippy. "I'll--"

"What is it?" cried Grace, springing up, shaking her head to more thoroughly awaken herself.

"Ah seen er man, Ah did," answered Washington. His eyes wore a frightened expression and he was shifting and shuffling uneasily. "Ah seen his face. He war a peekin' through the bushes right thar where yuh be sleepin'," he informed them, nodding to Lieutenant Wingate.

"You were dreaming," scoffed Hippy.

"Ah wuz wide awake, Cap'n. Er fly er a bug bit me on de nose an' waked me up. Ah seed de man den, an' when he seen I sawed him he run away."

"I hope you gave him an anesthetic before you 'sawed' him, Wash," said Emma Dean, who had been listening eagerly to the conversation.

"Yes'm."

Hippy started towards the spot indicated by Wash.

"Wait! Don't trample down the bushes until I have had a look," begged Grace, stepping forward. "We will look first."

Parting the bushes she peered in and pointed. Hippy saw a well-marked trail where the bushes had been brushed aside, and here and there a tender leaf-stem broken off.

Stooping over, the Overland girl scrutinized the ground, and, with a finger, beckoned Hippy to kneel down.

"See that?" she demanded.

"What is it?" questioned the other girls in chorus. They had followed Grace and Hippy and were eagerly peering over the heads of the two kneeling Overlanders.

"Footprints of a pair of heavy boots," announced Hippy. "The impression they have left in the moss is unmistakable. This looks as if he had rested his gun-butt here," he added, laying a finger on another depression in the moss.

"I do not think so," said Grace, after examining it critically. "I should say that the man made that second impression with the toe of his left boot. By looking at the impression of the right boot you will observe that it sunk in deeper, meaning, probably, that he threw his weight on the right foot and took a step forward with the left, only the toe of which was on the ground as he leaned forward to peer into our camp."

"'Ma'velous! Ma'velous, Sherlock!' How do you do it?" chortled Hippy.

"Elfreda, please fetch my revolver. I am going to follow out this trail a little way. Perhaps I may discover something," said Grace.

Hippy said he would accompany her, but Grace shook her head.

"Please stay here and look out for the camp. If I need you I will shoot three times."

"I wish you would not go out," urged Elfreda. "What is to be gained? Nothing, and there may be much to lose."

"Grace has made up her mind to go, so you might as well save your breath, J. Elfreda," said Anne.

"Some persons are so stubborn," murmured Emma.

Grace smiled and nodded, then parted the bushes and stepped in. She was lost to their sight in a few seconds, moving on through the tangle of bush and vine without causing a rustle that their listening ears could hear.

"Fine, fine!" observed Miss Briggs. "We surely have made a most excellent start."

"Cheer up. The worst is yet to come," reiterated Hippy. "Keep your ears open. I'll be back in a moment."

Hippy ran to his tent, returning with his heavy army revolver strapped to his waist.

"What are you going to do?" questioned Anne. "Grace said you were not to follow her."

"I'm not going to. I have merely prepared myself in case she signals for me. All hands keep quiet and listen. Stop that noise!" warned Hippy as Wash struck a chord on his harmonica. "Nora, if he sounds another note, take the infernal music box away from him. I--hark!"

A sharp report startled the Overland girls.

"That wasn't Grace's revolver," announced Lieutenant Wingate, leaning forward in a listening attitude, but before the words had left his lips, in fact, instantly following the first shot came a heavy report, a bang that woke the mountain echoes.

"That's Grace! That's a service revolver," cried Hippy.

"They're at it!" exclaimed Elfreda, as three more shots in quick succession, two of them from Grace's revolver, were fired.

"Run, Hippy!" cried Nora Wingate. "Shake your feet!"

"My knees are shaking already. Isn't that enough?" returned Hippy as he plunged into the bushes going to Grace's assistance, but there was nothing in his movements to indicate that his knees were shaking. Hippy Wingate knew no fear, as befitted a man who had fought many winning battles with the Germans high above the earth, but it amused him to convey the impression that he was timid.

# CHAPTER V
# THE WAY IS BARRED

The Overland Riders were calm. The thrilling experiences through which they had passed, while engaged in war work in France, had taught them to be so.

"Do--do you think--she is hurt?" stammered Emma.

"We sincerely hope not," answered Anne. "Judging from the reports, it was Grace who fired the last shot we heard," said Elfreda Briggs. "Still, that does not prove anything. I would suggest that we arm ourselves at once and prepare for trouble. There appears to be plenty of it abroad in these mountains."

Acting on her suggestion, the four girls hurried to their tents and armed themselves with rifles, then, taking positions around the outer edge of the camp, just within the bushes, they watched and waited, observed by Washington Washington with wide, frightened eyes.

It was Elfreda who made the first discovery. She caught the faint sound of some one moving through the bushes and raised her rifle.

"Halt! Who comes?" she demanded as she saw the bushes sway, a few yards ahead of her, as some one worked their way slowly through them.

"It's Grace," came the answer. "Help me in."

"Girls!" called Miss Briggs sharply, springing forward. She paused at the first glimpse of Grace Harlowe's face, which was pale; then hurried to her.

There were flecks of blood on Grace's cheek, and by that token Elfreda Briggs knew that she had been hit.

"Got a smack, I see."

"Just a mere scratch," replied Grace. "It made me feel weak and dizzy, but I shall be myself in a few moments."

Elfreda led her companion into the camp, then examined Grace's wound, which, as the Overland girl had said, was a mere scratch over the left temple. Miss Briggs washed the wound where a bullet had barely grazed the skin, and applied an antiseptic.

"Lie down a few minutes, Loyalheart," she urged.

Grace shook her head.

"I shall get my bearings sooner if I keep on my feet. I am ashamed of myself to give way to a little thing like a bullet scratch."

"That's because you're out of practice. You haven't been shot since last summer," said Emma Dean soothingly. "You won't mind it at all after you have been shot again a few times."

Grace laughed so merrily that, for the moment, she forgot the pain of her wound.

"Emma Dean, you are a regular tonic. I thank you. Now I am all right. Where is Hippy?" she questioned, gazing about her.

"Hippy!" wailed Nora Wingate. "Where is he?"

"He went out when we heard you shoot," Elfreda informed Grace. "Did he miss you?"

"I have not seen Hippy since I left this camp. He must have got lost," replied Grace. "Elfreda, fire three interval shots with your rifle to guide him in."

Miss Briggs did so, and all listened for an answer, but none came. Acting on Grace's suggestion, Elfreda fired further signal shots, and still no reply from Lieutenant Wingate.

Grace, finally becoming disturbed at Hippy's long absence, announced her intention of going out to look for him, and was giving her companions directions about signaling her when Hippy Wingate came strolling into camp, his clothing torn and his face scratched from contact with brier bushes. "Hulloa, folks," he greeted, grinning sheepishly.

"My darlin', my darlin', are you hurt?" cried Nora, hurrying to him solicitously.

"No. I got lost and just found myself. Where do you suppose I was? Why less than ten rods from this camp all the time. Never saw such a country for mixing a fellow up. Confound the whole business. If my property is in such a mess as this I'll set the lazy mountaineers at work clearing it up before I'll set foot on it. Hey! What hit you, Brown Eyes?"

"A bullet."

"I heard it. I mean I heard the shot, and, like the hero I am, I ran to the rescue, but got all tangled up," explained Hippy.

"Didn't you hear our shots?" demanded Anne.

"I heard 'em, but I was too busy untangling myself to answer. I thought the shots sounded off the other way and got deeper into the mess trying to find the camp."

"You are a fine woodsman," rebuked Elfreda.

"Yes, and you wouldn't be here yet had it not been for me," declared Emma Dean.

"How's that?" demanded Hippy.

"Well, you see, when we found that you did not come back and we surmised that you were lost, I just sat down and con-centrated. Then you came back, just like the cat did in the old story."

"Where did you get that piffle?" chortled Hippy when his laughter had subsided.

"From a professor who visited our town last winter. He said that, by con-centrating, one could bring anything to pass that he wished--provided he con-centrated intently enough and long enough. Why, he said that a person, by con-centrating properly, could move a house if he wished."

The Overlanders shouted.

"You'd better see a doctor," advised Hippy. "Brown Eyes, you haven't told me what happened to you. Who shot you?"

"I don't know. I did not see the person who did it. He saw me, evidently. Perhaps, catching a glimpse of my campaign hat, he thought it was you and shot at me. I let go at him, and we had it out. His second shot hit me and my third hit him. How badly I don't know, but he plainly had enough and got away without even picking up his rifle. It is out there yet, unless he returned for it."

"Did you follow him?" asked Nora.

"A few yards only, then I got dizzy and had to sit down for a few moments. That is all I know about it. I think we had better pack up and move."

"I sincerely hope the next stopping place may be more peaceful than those that have preceded it," said Miss Briggs.

"Please hurry, Washington," admonished Grace. "We have delayed much too long, and if we do not make haste we shall not reach our day's objective before dark. I don't fancy traveling here at night without a guide. Can you find your way about in the night, Washington?"

"Yes'm."

"I doubt it," observed Emma.

Soon after that, Grace now feeling fit again, the Overlanders were mounted and on their way, following a narrow trail, dodging overhanging limbs, pausing now and then to consult their map, for they had found that Washington could not be depended upon to guide them. He was useful, but apparently was not over-stocked with information about the mountains.

It was after seven o'clock that evening before they swung into a valley that, according to the map, narrowed into a cut in the mountains, through which ran a stream of sparkling water fed by equally sparkling mountain rivulets that rippled down to it in silver cascades. The Overland party was still riding under difficulties, for the trail was narrow and, in some instances, overgrown. They were now looking for the stream that the map indicated as being somewhere in the vicinity.

"Here's water," called Lieutenant Wingate, who was in the lead.

"Washington!" called Grace. "What is this stream?"

"Ah reckons it am watah," answered the colored boy, which brought a laugh from the Overlanders.

"Laundry must have been 'con-centrating,'" observed Anne Nesbit.

"This may be Spring Brook," called Miss Briggs. "We shall have to take for granted that it is."

"I think it is," answered Grace as they rode out into a fairly open space and discovered the cut in the mountains through which the stream was flowing.

The ponies already were showing their eagerness to wade into the water and drink, and Grace had just headed her mount towards the stream when she brought him up with a sharp tug on the bridle-rein.

Just ahead of her stood a tall, gaunt mountaineer leaning on his rifle. The expression on his face was not one of welcome, but Grace Harlowe saw fit to ignore that.

"Howdy, stranger," she greeted, smiling down at the man.

"Howdy," grunted the man, as they regarded each other appraisingly.

"Where do ye-all reckon yer goin'?" he demanded gruffly.

"Is this Spring Brook?" interjected Hippy.

"Ah reckon it air."

"Then that is where we are going."

"Yer kain't go this a-way," replied the mountaineer.

"Why can't we?" demanded Grace.

"'Cause Ah says ye kain't."

"Perhaps you do not know who we are. We are a party out for a ride through the Kentucky mountains. We ride every summer. We have no other object, and, if you will pause to consider, you will see that we can do no harm to you or any one else by going where we please in this part of the country," urged Grace.

"Ah knows who ye be. Turn aroun' an' git out o' here right smart!"

"You are making a mistake, sir," warned Grace. "If there is good reason why we should not go up this gorge we will go around it on the ridge."

"Ah said git out! Ye kain't go up the gorge nor over the ridge. Git out o' the mountains!"

"Not this evening, we won't!" shouted Lieutenant Wingate, now thoroughly angered, as he gathered up his reins.

**Bang!**

A bullet from the mountaineer's rifle went through the peak of Hippy Wingate's campaign hat, lifting it from his head and depositing it on the ground.

"Don't draw!" cried Grace in a warning voice as Hippy let a hand slip from the bridle-rein.

"Put yer hands up! All of ye!" commanded the mountaineer, the muzzle of his rifle swinging suggestively from side to side so as to cover the entire party.

## CHAPTER VI
## HIPPY MYSTERIOUSLY DISAPPEARS

All except Nora Wingate obeyed the command to hold up their hands.

"I'll not put me hands up for the likes of you!" she retorted, her eyes snapping, as she deliberately got down from her pony.

"Don't do anything foolish," warned Grace Harlowe.

Unheeding the warning, Nora stepped over and picked up Hippy's hat, eyed the hole in it, the color flaming higher and higher in her face. Nora then walked straight up to the mountaineer, apparently unconscious of the fact that his rifle was now pointed directly at her.

The mountaineer was nearer death at that moment than he knew, for two hands had slipped to two revolver butts resting respectively in the holsters of Grace Harlowe and Lieutenant Wingate. What mad thing Nora had in mind they could not imagine, but they did not believe the fellow would dare to shoot her down in cold blood, for it must be plain to him that she was unarmed.

"Look what you did!" she demanded, holding up the hat that the mountaineer might see the bullet hole in it. "You put a bullet through my husband's perfectly good hat. Aren't you ashamed of yourself? That hat cost him eight dollars, and if I thought you had eight dollars in the world, I'd make you pay for it. You're a cheap ruffian, that's what you are!"

Nora's chin was thrust out belligerently. At this juncture her right hand flashed up to the nose of the mountaineer. The fingers closed over that prominent member and Nora Wingate gave it a violent tweak.

The fellow's jaw sagged. He appeared actually dazed and the muzzle of his rifle, that Nora had thrust to one side as she boldly stepped up to him, had been permitted to sink slowly towards the ground.

Nora Wingate did not stop there. She soundly boxed the fellow's ears, first with the right, then with the left hand, each whack giving his head a violent jolt to one side.

"Jump back!" It was Grace Harlowe who, in an incisive tone of voice, gave the order to Nora.

"Why should I jump back?" demanded Nora, turning a flushed face to her companions. What she saw, however, caused Nora to take a few slow steps backwards. Three revolvers were pointed over her head at the mountaineer. The revolvers were in the hands of Grace Harlowe, Lieutenant Wingate and Elfreda Briggs.

The mountaineer saw the weapons at the same time.

"Drop it!" bellowed Hippy. "Drop it or I'll bore you full of holes!"

The mountain man permitted his grasp on his rifle to relax and the weapon fell to the ground.

"Back up!" commanded Hippy. "Don't play any tricks, and keep your hands away from your holster. Keep him covered, Grace, while I dismount. You, fellow! Take notice! We know how to shoot, probably better than you do. If you try any tricks you'll get what's coming to you. Turn around and stand still with your hands as high above your head as they will go. Good!"

Hippy dismounted and, with revolver at ready, stepped over to the man who was now standing with his back to the Overland Riders.

"Don't make a move! I'm going to take your revolver," warned Lieutenant Wingate, pressing his own revolver against the mountaineer's back. He then jerked the fellow's weapon from its holster and tossed it behind him. Nora picked it up.

"Turn around!"

The mountaineer faced him, his face contorted with deadly rage.

"I'll kill ye fer this 'ere!" threatened the man.

"Not this evening you won't. Listen to me, Mister Man. We are not here to interfere with you or with your business, and we wish to be let alone. So long as we are let alone, we shall move along peaceably. When we are not, some one is going to get hurt right smart. Get me?" Hippy thrust out his chin pugnaciously.

The mountaineer did not reply, but his eyes, and the malignant scowl on his face, voiced the thought that was uppermost in his mind.

"Now turn around, face up the gully and sprint when I give the word. Don't you show up in this vicinity until to-morrow. You will find your rifle and revolver right here where I am standing. We don't want any such antiquated hardware. Don't stop until you get to the other end of the gully, if you value your life. Go!"

The mountaineer started away at a brisk trot, never once looking behind him.

"Shoot! Make him dance," urged Emma Dean excitedly.

"No!" replied Grace incisively. "We are not savages."

"Why didn't you 'con-centrate' on him and save us all this bother?" demanded Hippy. "Nora darling, I am proud of you," he said, turning to her smilingly. "But never do a crazy thing like that again. Even Emma Dean could do no worse. What's the next thing on the programme, Grace? Do we go on or do we camp here?"

"I don't like the climate of Spring Brook at all. It is too warm and malarial for me," interjected Miss Briggs.

"I agree with you, J. Elfreda," replied Grace laughingly. "I would suggest that we detour to the right and proceed over the ridge, and on into the mountains where there may be a probability that we shall not be molested. What do you say, people?"

"I think we all agree with you," answered Anne.

"Yes, let's seek the seclusion of the mountain fastness and have Emma sit up and 'con-centrate' all night. If she can move a house and lot with her con-centration stunt, she surely should be able to move that touchy mountain savage further away from us," suggested Hippy to the discomfiture of Emma and the great amusement of her companions.

"I think you are real mean," pouted Emma.

"Would it not be a wise thing to do to leave one of us here for a short time to see if that fellow returns and tries to follow us?" asked Nora, still full of fight. "I should just like to teach him a lesson."

"You already have done so," chuckled Anne.

"Your suggestion is excellent," agreed Grace. "However, it is getting dark and we must locate ourselves before that. That is, we should do so. Let's go!"

The Overlanders then mounted and retraced their steps until they found a place where they could climb to the ridge. Reaching the top, they followed the ridge trail for half a mile, then struck off into the mountain fastness. In order to better hide their trail, they guided their horses into a small stream and rode up that for a full mile, finally finding a suitable camping place.

A cook fire, a small blaze, was made under a shelving rock, and Washington was left to cook the supper while Hippy and the girls watered and cared for the ponies. Supper was ready about the time they finished. The pitching of the tents was left for the boy to attend to while the Overlanders were eating.

"Now that we are composed, what does all this disturbance of to-day mean?" demanded Miss Briggs.

"It may be the result of our running that fellow out of our camp last night, or rather Hippy's running him out. Then again, the incident of to-day may be explained in another way. I first had a duel with some one in the bushes; later, when we headed into Spring Brook valley we may have been getting into the Moonshiners' territory. I understand they are rather touchy when it comes to outsiders penetrating their mountain preserves. At least this last savage was thoroughly in earnest when he ordered us to get out. I fear we should have gotten into trouble had it not been for Nora." Grace smiled at the recollection of Nora's chastisement of the mountaineer.

"Surely, they do not think we are revenue officers, do they?" asked Anne.

"They are suspicious of all strangers," Hippy informed his companions. "I had a friend in the flying corps, who comes from Kentucky, and he told me all about these mountaineers. They are, in a way, simple as children, but bad all through when they differ with you."

"Then, there is the Mystery Man," reminded Nora. "Is he one of them?"

"He may be for all we know about him," answered Elfreda, shrugging her shoulders.

Grace said "no."

"It doesn't seem probable, that, were he one of them, he would have shot one of them in our defense, does it?" she asked.

The Overlanders admitted the force of her argument. Supper finished, they sat about the campfire, now a glowing bed of coals, which now and then was fed and stirred into little ribbons of flame by adding bits of dry twigs.

"I am going to sit up to-night, and watch the camp," announced Hippy after the tents had been pitched and the girls, one by one, had begun to do their hair for the night.

"Yes, it will be wise. When you get sleepy, call me and I will take the watch for the rest of the night," directed Grace.

"I never sleep," remonstrated Hippy.

"He never sleeps," mimicked Emma in a deep voice from her tent, sending her companions into a shout of laughter.

"Except when he is supposed to be awake," teased Anne.

Before turning in, Grace made a circuit of the camp and the bushes and the trees surrounding it, halting where the ponies were tethered to see that they were properly tied for the night. Soon after making camp she had taken possession of Washington's harmonica, for it was all-important that attention be not attracted to their camp that night.

Grace was certain that they had not yet heard the last of their mountain enemies and that trouble might be looked for from that direction, hence no precaution must be overlooked with regard to protecting themselves.

"Tom was right," murmured Grace, when, after giving Washington and Hippy final directions, she had retired to her tent and lain down with rifle and revolver within easy reach.

Lieutenant Wingate put out the fire and sat down to watch, rifle in hand. Grace got up an hour later and, peering from her tent, saw Hippy sitting with his back against a rock. At first she thought he was asleep; then, when she saw him take off his hat and smooth back his hair, she knew that she was mistaken.

It was long past midnight when Grace again roused herself and got up with a feeling that all was not well. A quick survey of the camp from her tent revealed nothing disturbing. Hippy was in the same position in which she had seen him some hours before and not a sound was heard from the ponies' direction.

Picking up her rifle, and strapping on her revolver, Grace stepped over to Hippy and peered down into his face. He was sound asleep and snoring.

"It were a pity to wake him," she muttered, moving quietly away and sitting down within a dozen feet of the sleeping man to guard the camp for the rest of the night.

Grace suddenly tensed with every faculty on the alert. She thought she heard something moving cautiously in the bushes at the left of the camp. A few moments of listening convinced her that she was right. She knew that none of her outfit was out there and that Washington Washington was sleeping in his little pup-tent a few yards from her, for she could hear him breathing.

The Overland girl used her eyes and ears, and a few moments later she made out a vague form at the edge of the camp. Even then she would not have seen it, had it not moved to one side. The dark background prevented her being able to make anything out of the form, except that it was a human being.

Having satisfied herself of this, Grace raised her rifle, aiming it above the head of the intruder, and waited. Herself being in a deeper shadow, her movements were not observed by the prowler.

Grace put a gentle pressure on the trigger. A flash of fire and a deafening report followed.

Hippy Wingate sprang to his feet.

"Wha--wha--wha?" he gasped.

"Don't get excited," soothed the calm voice of Grace Harlowe. "I shot over the head of a prowler. Go back to your tent, Washington," she directed, as the colored boy ran out ready to bolt into the bushes.

Grace had heard the prowler crash through the bushes in his haste to get away, and felt reasonably certain that they would not be troubled by him again that night. In the meantime the others of her party had sprung from their tents, excitedly demanding to know what had occurred. She told them briefly, and advised that they go back to sleep.

"You too turn in, Hippy," directed Grace. "It is too bad to have spoiled that lovely sleep. I will look after the camp for the rest of the night."

Without a word Lieutenant Wingate went to his tent. He was ashamed of himself despite his former assertion that Nora Wingate always provided this emotion for him.

"I think I'll ask Emma to sit up and 'con-centrate' to keep me awake after this," muttered Hippy, and then lost himself in slumber.

The camp once more settled down and was not again disturbed, but Grace kept her vigil ceaselessly through the rest of the night. The girls did not know the details of the disturbance until breakfast next morning when Grace told them all she knew about the occurrence. After breakfast she and Hippy searched the ground about the camp and found traces of their visitor. In leaving he had made no effort to hide his trail, probably having been in too great a hurry, but Grace did not consider it worth while to try to follow the trail.

"We must make time, you know," she told her companions upon returning to camp. "If we are late in keeping our appointment with Tom, he will be worrying for fear something has happened to us."

"Something probably will have happened to us by that time," observed Elfreda solemnly. "Several somethings, perhaps."

After considerable milling about, after retracing their steps along the mountain rivulet, they found the trail that they were in search of, the footpath that led in the direction that they wished to go. On either side of the path was a jungle-like tangle of shrub and vine, through which the party, riding in single file, were obliged to force their way.

So dense was the foliage that they could not see each other, but they kept up a rattling fire of conversation back and forth, much of which was directed at Hippy who was leading and doing his best to beat down a path for those who were following. This continued for some time, until finally Hippy's mount seemed to be getting lazy, for Elfreda, who was riding directly behind the leader, bumped into his pony several times.

"Come, come, Hippy! Have you gone to sleep?" demanded Elfreda. "We shall never get out of the tangle at this rate."

There was no reply, and when Elfreda communicated her belief to her companions that Hippy had gone to sleep on his saddle, there was much laughter. Emma called out that, so long as the horse kept awake, they would be all right.

This condition of affairs continued for some little time, until finally Elfreda rode out into a rugged, rocky clearing and made a discovery that, for the moment, left her speechless.

Hippy Wingate's pony was browsing at tender blades of grass that were sprouting from crevices in the rocks, but its saddle was empty.

"Hippy! Oh, Hippy!" called Miss Briggs.

There was no response to her call. The pony raised its head and looked at her and then resumed its eating.

"Grace!" cried Elfreda in a tone that thrilled every member of the party. "Hurry! Hippy has gone!"

## CHAPTER VII
## A VOICE FROM THE SHADOWS

The Overlanders came trotting into the clearing, Grace bringing up the rear of the line just ahead of Washington and his mules, who still were some little distance behind.

"What is it?" called Grace as she burst into the clearing.

Miss Briggs pointed to Hippy's empty saddle, and it was not until then that Nora Wingate fully realized the meaning of the scene.

"Hippy, my darlin', where are you?" she cried excitedly.

"Steady now," cautioned Grace. "It will profit us not at all to lose our heads. Spread out and search the clearing. First, tie your ponies so they don't disappear and leave us in the lurch."

The girls quickly slipped from their saddles and began searching, Grace first having examined the saddle of Hippy's pony. She found his rifle in the saddle-boot and his revolver in the holster suspended from the pommel. This discovery indicated to her that Lieutenant Wingate had not had time to take either weapon with him when he dismounted.

"It is my opinion that Hippy fell asleep and fell off," declared Emma, after they had completed their search of the clearing.

"Oh, what shall we do?" wailed Nora, wringing her hands. "Grace darlin', help me think. I can't think straight. Somebody suggest something."

"When did you first discover that his pony was lagging?" questioned Grace, turning to Miss Briggs.

"I should say that it was twenty or thirty minutes ago."

"Say half a mile back. It is possible that Hippy was unseated by coming in contact with an overhanging limb, though I do not recall having seen any low enough to bump one's head."

"We must go back and try to find him," said Miss Briggs.

"Yes," agreed Grace, her brow puckering in thought. "Anne, I think you had better remain here in charge of the camp. Get your rifles out and be on the alert. This affair looks suspicious to me. Shoot a signal if you need us in a hurry. Elfreda, will you go with me?"

Miss Briggs nodded.

"Bring your revolver. Rifles will be in the way," advised Grace. "You girls stay right here. Do not attempt to leave this spot. Nora, keep your head level. Let's go!"

The two girls started back over the trail on foot, walking briskly. A short distance back from the clearing they met Washington, whom Grace directed to go on and wait for them in the clearing. She did not think it worth while to ask the boy if he had seen Lieutenant Wingate.

"I have a recollection of seeing the bushes trampled down on the left side of the trail as we came along," said Grace, after they had left Washington. "It is possible that there is where Hippy was unhorsed."

"Grace, you suspect something, don't you?"

"I don't know whether I do or not. I will tell you after we have found the place where he left the trail. Does not Hippy's disappearance strike you as being a strange one, Elfreda?" questioned Grace, giving her companion a quick glance of inquiry.

"Yes."

"I think we are nearing the spot to which I referred. Keep your eyes open and move slowly. Should we find nothing there, we will walk along a little way off the trail, each taking a side. There!"

Grace pointed to a spot where the bushes had been lately crushed down. She then laid a restraining hand on her companion's arm, and there they stood for a few moments, fixing the picture of the scene in their minds.

Grace finally parted the bushes and looked in, Miss Briggs peering over her shoulders. Using extreme caution they stepped into the bushes, to one side of the disturbed spot, and there Grace got down on her knees and examined the ground with infinite pains. She then crawled along a short distance, following the trail that had been made by whoever had passed through there.

"How far are you going?" asked Elfreda.

"I don't know."

Grace's search led her a full five hundred yards into the thicket, she halting only when she came to a spot where the brush had been trampled down over several yards of space. The sound of a stream could be heard close at hand.

An examination of the ground there gave Grace a fresh clue, and, after stepping over to the brook and gazing at it briefly, she announced herself as ready to go back.

"What now?" asked Elfreda.

"After I get something we will return to camp. We must hold a consultation. I do not feel like deciding this problem alone."

"I know you have made a discovery, but beyond the fact that some one has trampled down the bushes beside the trail, and that a horse has been standing where we are now, I must confess that I am no wiser than before."

"You have done very well," smiled Grace. "Come with me and I will enlighten you further."

They walked briskly back to the edge of the trail where they had first found the bushes disturbed.

"Two men have stood here. If you will scrutinize the ground you will see the imprint of their hobnailed boots. They stood facing each other, just as you and I are doing at this moment. All at once they turned facing the trail and took a step toward it."

"Wait a moment! Wait a moment! You are going too fast for me, Grace Harlowe. Are you gifted with second sight that you know all this?"

"J. Elfreda, for goodness' sake use your eyes. The footprints are so plain that all you have to do, to understand, is to look at them. They tell the whole story up to a certain point," answered Grace.

"Go on."

"They unhorsed Hippy at that point, and I should not be at all surprised if they hit him over the head with a club or the butt of a revolver. You see how easy it would be to do that without being discovered, the foliage being so dense over the trail. After unhorsing him they at least dragged him back for some little distance before they picked him up. I found the marks of his heels where they had dug into the soft earth as he was being dragged."

"You--you said you wished to--to get something," reminded Miss Briggs, somewhat dazed by her companion's rapid recital.

"Yes. I discovered it when I was on my knees examining the trail here." Grace stooped over and, thrusting a hand into the bushes, brought forth an object which she held up for Elfreda's inspection.

"Do you recognize it, J. Elfreda?"

"Hippy's hat!" gasped Miss Briggs.

"Yes. Let us examine it. Look at this! Am I right?" demanded Grace triumphantly. "Hippy was whacked over the head with the butt of a revolver, and the blow cut right through the felt. No wonder he made no outcry. He is a lucky fellow if he hasn't a fractured skull. Elfreda, this is serious."

"Both serious and marvelous--serious so far as Hippy is concerned, and marvelous so far as your visualizing the incident is concerned," declared Miss Briggs.

"Do you think we should tell Nora?"

"We must tell her something, and we cannot tell her an untruth," replied Elfreda after brief reflection. "I should advise telling her all except about the hat. We can conveniently forget about the hat. He was taken prisoner by two men, probably in the belief that it was some one else they were capturing."

"I don't think so," interrupted Grace.

"I do," insisted Miss Briggs.

"All right, then you tell the story to Nora. Let's go back."

Grace hid the hat, intending to return for it at another time, as it might be useful as evidence. They then started on to join their companions, both silent and thoughtful.

Reaching the halting place of the party in the clearing, Elfreda, without giving Grace an opportunity to speak, launched forth into a description of what they had discovered--minus the hat.

Nora wept silently, and Emma slipped a comforting hand into hers.

"Don't cry, Nora darling. Hippy will be back. Nobody, not even a mountaineer, could live with him very long. I don't see how you ever stood it so long as you have." Saying which, Emma prudently dropped the hand she was holding, and backed away.

Nora Wingate sprang up blazing, to meet the laughing eyes and impishly uptilted nose of the irrepressible Emma Dean. Nora laughed and wept at the same time, and then quickly pulled herself together.

"I ought to take ye over me knee, but I won't because ye've brought me to me senses. Grace, see how calm I am. I am ready to listen to your plan, knowing very well that you have one in mind. If they haven't killed him, my Hippy will yet beat those scoundrels at their own game. Any man who has fought duels with the Germans above the clouds, and won, surely will be able to outwit a whole army of these thick-headed mountaineers. What do you think we should do?"

"At the beginning of this journey, as well as those we have taken before, it was agreed between us that when one strays away or gets separated from the party, the Overlanders were to go into camp at or as near the point of separation as possible, and wait there a reasonable time for the return of the absent one. That is what I should suggest doing in the present instance," offered Grace.

"Make camp right here?" asked Anne.

"Yes."

"Yes, but are we not going to try to find my Hippy?" begged Nora.

"I think it advisable to wait a reasonable time, so, with the approval of you folks, I will tell Washington to make camp."

This the girls agreed to, though Nora was for setting out in search of her husband at once. That, too, was what Grace Harlowe would have liked to do, but she believed it would be better for them to remain where they were for the time being.

"Couldn't you follow the trail of those men?" asked Nora.

"I did up to the point where they rode into a stream to throw off pursuers, just as we did last night. Of course they had to leave the stream somewhere, but the probabilities are that they were sharp enough not to leave a plain trail where they came out. For instance, they could easily dismount their prisoner on a rocky footing where no trail would be left, carry him on and secrete him, then have one of their party ride the horses in another direction. Don't you see where that would leave us?"

"Oh, yes, I do," moaned Nora. "My wheels are all turning the wrong way. Don't mind me."

"We won't," promised Emma.

Washington, aroused from a day dream, was directed to hustle himself and make camp. While he was busying himself at this, the girls held a further conference. At its conclusion, Grace paid another visit to the scene of Lieutenant Wingate's undoing.

This time, Grace followed the trail left by the two men who had captured him, and then on down the stream until she came in sight of a rocky clearing, where she believed the captors had left the brook and followed out the plan that she had visualized.

Grace dared not press her investigation further, nor even show herself, the Overland girl shrewdly reasoning that the spot would be watched by those responsible for Hippy's disappearance. She was not desirous of taking unnecessary chances just yet, for, being the captain of her party, she was responsible for their safety.

All during the rest of the day, after her return to camp, one or the other of the girls was posted outside the camp, secreted in the bushes, to prevent a surprise by intruders. So far as they could discover no one approached the camp.

The camp having been pitched at the extreme end of the open space, the campfire, at Elfreda's suggestion, was built at the opposite end, which, as she pointed out, would leave their tents in a shadow after dark, for there were a few scattering laurel bushes between the tents and the fire, but not so dense that the view was greatly interfered with.

The outside guarding was continued until nearly bedtime, eyes and ears being strained, not only for prowlers, but for the return of Hippy Wingate.

"If we get no word to-morrow, what?" questioned Anne.

"Grace and myself will take the trail," announced Elfreda. "If she does not think it wise to go, I can go alone."

"We will both go, unless something occurs to make our going inadvisable," answered Grace quietly. "Elfreda, you and I will sit up together to-night, if you don't mind."

After the others had turned in and Washington had piled some hard wood on the fire, so that a bed of coals might remain for some hours after the flames had died out, Grace and Elfreda sat down together in the shadows near the tents and began their long night's vigil.

Their conversation was pitched too low to be heard by one a yard away; in fact it was carried on mostly in whispers.

Elfreda's watch showed that it lacked but a few minutes of one when, as she gazed at the illuminated dial, Grace suddenly gripped her arm.

"I heard something in the bushes," whispered Grace. "It may have been an animal. I rather think it was. I--"

Something thudded on the ground between the two girls and the laurel shrubs.

"Wha--at is it?" whispered Grace.

"A stick of wood," replied Elfreda. "It looks like a section of a tree limb. Something white is wrapped about it. Oughtn't we to see what it is?"

"No!" answered Grace with emphasis. "Sit tight. It may be a trick."

With rifles held at ready, ears alert, Elfreda Briggs and Grace Harlowe sat almost motionless until the skies began to assume a leaden gray that foretold the coming of another day.

A few moments later Elfreda crept over and returned with the stick that she had observed to fall. An old newspaper sheet was wrapped about it. This Miss Briggs undid cautiously, Grace's eyes keenly observing the operation.

"Look! There is writing on the lower margin of the sheet," she said.

Miss Briggs turned the page around and eagerly read the words that were penciled there.

"'Stay where you are. Friends are working in your
behalf. In the meantime guard yourselves
vigilantly.

'A FRIEND.'"

The message that Elfreda had read out loud to her companion served to deepen the mysteries that surrounded them, yet, as they pondered and discussed it, the message seemed to convey to them the hope that at least one of the mysteries might soon be solved.

# CHAPTER VIII
# A FRIEND IN NEED

"Hey! What hit me?" demanded Hippy Wingate, opening his eyes.

"Keep shet!" commanded a surly voice near at hand.

Hippy tried to raise his arms, but could not. They were roped to his sides, as he discovered now that he was regaining full consciousness. A dim light filtering through an opening that he could not see, for it was behind him, showed Lieutenant Wingate that he was lying in one of the shallow caves that may be found almost anywhere in the Kentucky mountains.

"How did I--I get here?" he ventured to ask.

The other occupant of the cave stepped up and gave the captive a vicious prod with his boot.

"Ouch! Say, you! Don't be so infernally rough about it. Kicking is a dangerous habit to get into. One of these days you will forget yourself and kick a Kentucky mule. Then *good night*!"

"Didn't Ah tell ye-all to keep still? Want another clip ovah the haid?"

"Thank you, no," replied Hippy. "If you don't mind, before I relapse into gloomy silence, you might tell me what the big idea is. Who or what hit me, and why am I here hog-tied like a captured hoss thief?"

"Mebby ye-all be that. Kain't answer no questions, an' if ye don't keep still Ah'll shoot ye. Ah reckon ye-all will keep still that-away."

"Ah reckon maybe you're right," agreed Hippy, and was silent.

Lieutenant Wingate was kept in the cave all that day. Now and then his guard would go out for a short time, and, returning, would stand peering down at the prisoner, but no further conversation passed between them.

Hippy tried to recall what had happened to him. He remembered riding along the trail; remembered the good-natured teasing of the Overland girls, then all at once consciousness was blotted out. He had a faint recollection of being jolted, which probably was when he was being carried away on a horse, but that was the extent of his recollections. He did know that his head hurt him terribly and that it felt twice its natural size. His throat was parched from thirst, but Lieutenant Wingate declared to himself that he would die rather than ask a favor of the ruffian there who was guarding him.

Shortly after dark Hippy heard voices outside the cave; then two men came in, jerked him to his feet and, dragging him out, threw him over the back of a pony just ahead of the saddle, as if he were a bag of meal. When the rider mounted, Hippy was placed right side up on the saddle, his companion sitting behind him on the horse's back.

A rough, miserable ride of something more than an hour followed; then they halted. Hippy, now being blindfolded, could make out nothing of his surroundings, but he realized that there were trees all about him, and he could hear the snapping of a campfire, which reminded him of food and that he was nearly famished.

"If they fry bacon near enough for me to smell, I'll break my bonds and run-- for the bacon," he added to himself.

Lieutenant Wingate was roughly yanked from the horse. He landed heavily on the ground in a heap, where he was left to untangle himself as best he could. By violent winking and twisting his head from side to side he was able, by tilting his head well back, to displace the handkerchief with which he had been blindfolded sufficiently to enable him to look about.

Several men were holding a discussion by the campfire, and that their conversation had to do with him, Hippy Wingate knew from the frequent gestures in his direction, though he was too far away to distinguish what they were saying.

The men finally came over to him and demanded to know who and what he was.

Hippy told them briefly. One of the men laughed.

"Ye mean ye'r a hoss thief," he jeered.

"I wish I were. I'd steal a horse and get away from here."

"Know anybody in these parts, anybody who'll give ye a character?" questioned another.

"No. I've got a character of my own. I don't need any one to give me a character," retorted Hippy.

"Who is the feller that come inter these mountains with ye, and then quit ye in such a hurry?" demanded another.

"His name is Tom Gray. He is the husband of Grace Harlowe Gray, who leads our party of Riders. He has gone over to the Cumberlands on business."

"Whut business?"

"He is to make a survey for the government."

Lieutenant Wingate had let slip something that he should not have done. He saw instantly from the exclamations that the mountaineers uttered under their breaths, that he had "said something," as he expressed it to himself.

"So that's it, hey! Be ye-all workin' fer the gov'ment, too?" demanded a voice.

"I am not, nor have I been since I fought in France. Is there anything else that you ruffians wish to have me tell you?" demanded Hippy belligerently.

"Where be the other feller headed for fust?"

"I don't know where he is headed for now," answered the captive, becoming wary.

"Reckon we'd better look that gov'ment feller up right smart," said one of the captors in a low tone. "We'll bag the bunch of 'em. Shore ye ain't got nothin' else t' tell us honest folk up here?" demanded the first speaker.

"No."

"Reckon ye better think it over, young feller. We'll give ye till ter-morrer t' make a clean sweep an' tell us the whole business. If ye don't we'll jest blow yer fool haid off an' chuck ye in a hole in the mountain an' there won't be nothin' more heard of ye," threatened another.

"The Germans tried to do that same thing, but they didn't succeed," dared Lieutenant Wingate. "Who do you think I am, anyway? What do you think I am? Come, now, suppose you make a clean sweep and tell me what all this rotten business is about."

"Ah reckons ye don't have t' be told nothin'," was the reply that Hippy got. "We're goin' t' take ye away from here an' put a guard over ye, so if ye wants t' live till ter-morrer, keep quiet."

"Wait a moment!" called Hippy, as the captors turned away for further conference. "Don't I get anything to eat out of all this?"

There was no reply to his question, and Hippy went without his supper, which fact really gave him more concern than the knowledge that he was a prisoner in the hands of desperate men, who, if their word could be believed, proposed to do desperate things to him.

All but two of the mountaineers soon left the scene, and these two took turns in sleeping and guarding their prisoner. Along towards morning Hippy fell into an uneasy sleep, but his sleep was brief. He was roughly yanked to his feet, and, at the point of a rifle, driven deeper into the forest. His guards did not halt until daybreak. They then untied the prisoner's arms, bound his feet, and placing him in a sitting position, back against a tree, passed a rope around his waist and tied him to the tree.

"You forgot something," reminded Hippy as they started to walk away.

"Huh?" demanded one of the mountaineers.

"You forgot to tie the tree down. It might run away, you know."

A grunt was the only reply he got. The men then built a small fire and began preparing their breakfast. Bacon and coffee was their meal, and Hippy Wingate, now without his blindfold, was forced to sit there and watch them eat. It was the most unhappy hour that he remembered ever to have experienced.

After finishing their own breakfast they favored him with a cup of water, and, lighting their pipes, sat down to talk, much of which the listening ears of their captive overheard.

As nearly as Hippy could make it out a mountain feud was in the making, and the twenty-third of the month was the time set for the opening. He heard the names "Bat Spurgeon" and "Jed Thompson" mentioned, but they conveyed nothing to him beyond the mere names. The voices of his captors and his own weariness finally lulled Lieutenant Wingate to sleep, and he slept for hours. He was awakened late in the day by being roughly shaken and a cup of water thrust into his hands.

"I thank you for this bounteous repast," said Hippy mockingly. "Is this the water cure you are giving me?"

"Oh, shut up!" growled the mountaineer, and went away leaving Hippy gazing after him, a sardonic grin on the Overland Rider's face.

Hippy was aching all over his body as darkness settled over the forest, marking the second night of his captivity. With it came the cook fire and again the agonizing odors of coffee and bacon. With it, too, came something else--a low, guarded voice behind him and, seemingly, only a few inches from his ear.

"Don't make a sound, Lieutenant."

"Who are you?" demanded Hippy, without in the least changing his position or showing excitement.

"You would not know if I told you. Listen to me. When those two fellows sit down to supper, the light of the fire will be in their eyes, and, unless they get up and stare, they will not be able to see you in this shadow. If everything is safe I will cut you loose. Are your feet bound?"

"Yes. Who are you?"

"You wouldn't know if I told you, I said. Keep quiet and speak only in answer to my questions."

"All right. Got anything loose about your person--I mean food, man-sized food, not canary-bird rations such as those bandits have been doling out to me?"

"You can't have anything now. After we have gotten away from here I will try to dig up a snack for you. Silence!"

For the next several minutes neither the prisoner nor his mysterious friend uttered a word. Supper was ready for the mountaineers, but, before sitting down to it, one of them walked over to the prisoner and stood peering down at him. Hippy's heart almost stopped beating, so intent was he on listening for the breathing of the man behind him and from his fear that his mysterious friend might be discovered.

No such emergency arose, nor did he hear the breathing he was listening for.

After satisfying himself that the captive was safe, the mountaineer returned to the fire and sat down to his supper.

Hippy felt a slight tug on the rope that bound him, then its pressure about his waist was released.

"Steady, now," warned that even voice behind him. "Crawl on all fours."

The rescuer placed a hand on Hippy's shoulder and guided him slowly, cautiously, every movement forward threatening to draw a groan from the released captive.

"Now get up! Give me your hand," whispered, the stranger. "Don't speak."

For some little time they crept on in silence, the stranger twisting and turning, finally taking to the middle of a mountain stream and following it up for some distance when he halted.

"Tell me what the situation is back there. What did they propose to do to you?" demanded the man.

"I expect the gang is on its way there now to shoot me up, provided I do not give them the information they seek," answered Hippy.

"What information?"

Lieutenant Wingate repeated the conversation of the previous night, leaving out no details, however trivial they might seem to him.

"I thought so. Come up here and sit down. I shall have to leave you, perhaps for an hour or more. When I return I will give one short whistle. If all is well you will reply with two short whistles."

"You are going back there to spy on that outfit that we just left?" questioned Hippy.

"Yes. I want to see who the others are, and what they have up their sleeves. Here's a revolver for you. I suppose they took yours. Don't use it unless you have to."

"Wait a moment!" called Hippy, as his mysterious friend started away. "Haven't you forgotten something? That 'snack' you promised to dig for."

"Oh, yes. Here's some dog biscuit for you, and--"

"Dog biscuit?" exclaimed Hippy.

"Hardtack. You ought to know what that is," chuckled the stranger.

Hippy groaned. It revived painful memories of France in wartime, but he accepted the hardtack and began biting it off in large chunks. Hippy did not concern himself about how long the mysterious friend remained away so long as the biscuit held out, unpalatable as it was.

"I shall be listening for shells to burst first thing I know. Army food! How did I ever eat it for nearly two years and live?"

It was full two hours later when the welcome whistle signal sounded somewhere down stream, which Lieutenant Wingate answered as directed.

"Come! We will head for your camp now," announced the man a few moments later, as he stepped up before Hippy.

"Did you learn anything on your little excursion?" questioned Hippy thickly, for his mouth was well filled with hardtack.

"Yes, Lieutenant. I learned a great deal. I was there when the crowd came in to put you on the rack. The two fellows who let you get away had a hard time of it, and it looked for a time as if there was going to be shooting. Cooler heads, however, headed it off. When you get back to your party I should advise you to pull up stakes and get out. Those fellows will be after you and you'll have to look alive or you won't be alive long."

"I know I am thick, old man, but tell me why they are so eager to blow my light out," begged Hippy.

"Don't you know, Lieutenant?"

"If I did I shouldn't be asking you. Begging your pardon for my bluntness."

"One reason, but not the principal one, is that you bounced one of the gang from your camp."

"Go on. What's the big idea?"

"The big idea, as you call it, is that there is a price on your head up here! Now do you understand, Lieutenant?"

Hippy Wingate uttered a low, long-drawn whistle of amazement.

# CHAPTER IX
# THE POWER OF MIND

What do you suppose it can mean, and who threw it into our camp?" wondered Elfreda Briggs, folding up the newspaper that contained the message to them.

"It must mean that a friend is interested in our welfare," replied Grace. "Whoever and whatever he may be, his advice is good, and here we stay until we find Hippy. I am going out right after breakfast and make an effort to pick up the trail. Surely the outlaws, or whatever they are, will not be waiting all that time for us to follow them. I will make a quiet scout. I do not look to be interfered with, for they surely will have gone away by now."

"Shall I call the girls and tell them? The knowledge that a helping hand has been held out to us surely will comfort Nora," said Elfreda.

"Yes. I will rout out Washington and have him start the fire. It has been a trying night and I am glad it is at an end," replied Grace.

"I knew it," cried Emma Dean when she learned what had taken place. "I didn't con-centrate for nothing."

"You what?" frowned Elfreda.

"I have been con-centrating all night long--con-centrating on Hippy to call him back to us."

"Oh, you darlin'," cried Nora, throwing her arms about Emma.

"I should advise you to continue to 'con-centrate,'" suggested Anne. "If you were to stop now you might break the mental string; then we should lose Hippy for good."

"You just wait. You'll see whether or not he comes back," retorted Emma indignantly.

Nora's face was flushed that morning and her heart was filled with a new hope--the hope that Hippy might be with them before the close of that day.

After breakfast, as planned, Grace took up her rifle and went away, leaving Elfreda and the others to guard the camp and, incidentally, to keep Washington busy and out of mischief. He was, too, forbidden to play his harmonica lest the noise attract attention to the camp of the Overland Riders.

Proceeding cautiously, Grace reached the stream, and followed it until she found where the kidnappers of Hippy had left it. After waiting and watching for a full hour, Grace stepped out boldly. For six hours the Overland girl employed all her knowledge of the open in an effort to pick up the trail of the mountaineers, but the trail appeared to end abruptly at the bank of the creek. Not even the hoofprints of horses could be found on the softer ground a short distance back from the stream.

There are tricks in masking one's trail that the Kentucky mountaineers had learned from generations of feuds and attacks by revenue agents, which Grace Harlowe knew nothing of.

At noon she gave up the attempt to find the trail over which Hippy Wingate had been taken, and started back towards the camp.

"What luck?" called Nora, as she appeared at the edge of the clearing where the camp was pitched.

"None. As a trailer, I am a miserable failure, a rank amateur."

"If you were to spend as much time con-centrating as you do tearing about over the landscape, you would be more successful," declared Emma wisely, at which there was a laugh at Grace's expense.

"I surely could not be more unsuccessful than I have been," replied Grace smilingly.

The afternoon was passed in discussing their situation. While the girls were eager to be out trying to find Hippy, they believed that they were doing the wise thing in following the advice of their unknown friend, whose message had been tossed into their camp, so they remained in camp and waited.

When night came and still no Hippy, the depression of the Overlanders increased and there was little conversation, each one appearing to be listening, Emma, with a faraway look in her eyes, now and then relapsing into deep thought. Emma was "con-centrating."

The same arrangement for guarding the camp, as had been carried out the previous night, was again followed. This time, Grace took one side of the camp and Miss Briggs the other. Both hid in deep shadows, each with a rifle at her side and a revolver in its holster. Thus prepared they settled themselves for the night, all the other members of the party being in their tents and, supposedly, asleep.

It was late when Grace and Elfreda were aroused by Washington talking, muttering in his sleep, then the nerves of the two girls leaped to attention as, out of the bushes on Miss Briggs' side of the camp, a twig snapped. It was accompanied by a sound that indicated the presence of a human being.

"Who goes?" demanded Elfreda sharply.

*Bang!*

Without giving the maker of the noise out there time to answer, she fired a shot from her revolver into the trees in that direction, but high enough to be certain that one underneath them would not be hit.

Miss Briggs' shot brought instant results.

"Hey there! Cut the gun!" howled Hippy Wingate.

"It's Hippy!" breathed Grace, springing to her feet. "Don't shoot, Elfreda!"

The two girls sprang up and waited. They were still cautious, but their companions, awakened by the shot, were not. Nora, Anne and Emma rushed out, demanding excitedly to know what the trouble was.

At this juncture Hippy walked into the clearing.

"Meet me with a pail of food! I'm starving!" he wailed.

For the next few minutes there was excitement in the camp, Nora clinging to Hippy's neck laughing and crying, Emma standing a little aloof from them with a superior smile on her face, Anne, urging the wide-eyed Washington to start the fire and prepare coffee, and Grace seeking to quiet Nora so that they might hear Hippy's story.

When the campfire blazed up and they saw his condition, Nora wept again. Hippy was hatless--his hat was out in the bushes where Grace, after finding it, had secreted it--his clothes were torn, he was hollow-eyed, and his head wore a lump that stood out prominently.

"Never mind the trimmings. Give me food," he begged. Then between mouthfuls he told the story of his capture so far as he knew it, told it to the moment of his reaching the Overland camp. Hippy said he intended, if possible, to creep in quietly without awakening any one and give the girls a big surprise in the morning, when Elfreda threw a wrench into the machinery, "and tried to wing me," he added amid laughter.

"I could not afford to wait," answered Miss Briggs.

"You sure are some quick on the trigger," declared Hippy. "The fellow who was with me ducked, and I heard him chuckling and laughing as he sneaked away."

"Yes, but, had it not been for me, you might not have been here, Lieutenant Wingate," interjected Emma Dean.

"Eh? How's that, Emma?"

"Why, I--I con-centrated on you and brought you back," answered Emma solemnly.

"What a pity," murmured Hippy sadly. "And she so young."

"Who was the man who rescued you?" questioned Grace, after the laugh at Emma's expense had subsided.

"I don't know. I never saw him before. He is a slick article, whoever he may be."

"Are you certain that it was not our Mystery Man?" asked Anne.

"I am. Say! We must get out of here right smart, for there is going to be trouble," urged Hippy.

"I should say that we already have had our share of it," complained Elfreda.

"Yes, but this is different, child. The mountaineers are after us--after me especially," he added, throwing out his chest a little.

"After you--after you, Hippy, my darlin'?" cried Nora. "Why should they be after you?"

"I don't know any more about it than you do. Perhaps the little mix-ups we had with those two fellows may have something to do with it."

"It must be something more serious than revenge for your having bounced one and driven the other one away," offered Grace. "Will you please tell me why we should move in such a hurry?"

"Because the fellow who got me out of my scrape said we must. He says we have got to make Thompson's farm as quickly as possible and stay there until the storm blows over," insisted Lieutenant Wingate. "Of course, I don't give a rap for myself, but I have a great moral responsibility."

"A what?" interjected Emma.

"Moral responsibility. I am responsible for the safety of you girls and my powerful body shall stand between you and all harm."

"Ahem--m--m," piped Emma Dean.

"To what storm did he refer?" asked Grace. She was regarding Hippy narrowly, not yet sure that he was not joking, though she did not believe he was.

"I don't know, Brown Eyes. That depends upon which way the wind blows. It feels like snow to me. He did not say what kind of storm, but he strongly advised what I have told you," answered the lieutenant.

"It doesn't sound reasonable to me. I do not see how we should be any safer on the farm you speak of, than we shall be by following the trail to Hall's Corners, all the time attending strictly to our own business," observed Elfreda.

"Nor do I," agreed Grace.

"I will tell you why, Elfreda," answered Hippy. "We shall be safer there, where, for some reason, my informant doesn't seem to think those ruffians will bother us. Whereas, if we remain out and continue on our way to our destination, I shall probably be shot. Those mountaineers are bound to get me."

"What?" gasped Nora Wingate. "Hippy, my darlin', do you mean it?"

"Yes I do. There is a price on my head up here! That's the whole story."

"A price! Huh! If there is, I'll wager that it is a cut-rate price. Good-night! I am going back to bed." Emma Dean turned her back on them and flounced off to her tent.

# CHAPTER X
## "THEY'VE GOT THE BOY"

I don't believe it. Your rescuer was drawing the long bow," spoke up Anne Nesbit.

"Yes, I can't imagine Hippy with a price on his head," nodded Miss Briggs.

"When I'm dead you folks will be sorry that you didn't take me seriously," rebuked Lieutenant Wingate. "Do we do as my friend suggested, and hike for the Thompson farm, or must I be sacrificed on the altar of unbelief?"

"Grace must answer that question. She is our captain," answered Elfreda.

Grace Harlowe regarded Hippy with searching eyes.

"You are not fooling us, Hippy?" she demanded.

"Could I be so base as to deceive my dearest friends?" answered Lieutenant Wingate in an aggrieved tone. "How can you doubt me?"

"Girls, if there be no objection, we will start at daybreak. Washington, do you know where the Thompson farm is?" questioned Grace.

"Ah reckon Ah does," drawled Washington.

"How far is it from here?"

"'Bout two skips an' er jump, Ah reckons."

"He thinks we are a flock of fleas," grumbled Hippy under his breath.

"I will get the map. We shall learn nothing from Washington," said Grace, rising. "Washington, pack up everything we shall not need to-night. We wish to make an early start in the morning."

"Yes'm."

Fetching the map, Grace and Elfreda pored over it and finally located the farm in question. The map was a sectional map issued by the government and gave every trail and landmark in the territory that it covered.

"I should say Thompson's farm is about twenty miles from here. It appears to be quite a bit out of our way, but that doesn't matter in the circumstances. Yes, I think we can make it. All right, Hippy."

"What about to-night?" asked Miss Briggs.

"The same arrangement as last night," replied Grace in a low tone. "We will take turns. Take your blanket out. He needs a rest to-night," nodding towards Hippy Wingate.

Neither Grace nor Elfreda felt like sitting up another night. Hippy insisted that he must take his watch on guard, but they declined his offer, telling him that they could not trust him to keep awake in view of what he had been through and the sleep he had lost. So the two girls took up their vigil again, Grace lying down near her companion, Elfreda taking the first watch of the night.

It was not long after the camp had settled down to sleep that Elfreda put a quick pressure on the arm of her companion. Grace was awake instantly.

"What is it?" she whispered, instinctively sensing that the pressure on her arm was a warning pressure.

"I thought I heard something yonder by Washington's tent," whispered Miss Briggs.

"Yes, something is moving about there," agreed Grace, after a few minutes of attentive listening. "It may be Washington himself. Don't shoot. Remember, too, that the ponies are in that direction, so if we have to fire we must fire high."

"I had thought of that. I--"

Miss Briggs was interrupted by the most unearthly yell that any member of the Overland party had ever heard. The yell was uttered by Washington Washington.

"Leggo me! Leggo! He kotched me! He kotched me! Wo--o--o--o--o--ow!"

The howls of the colored boy ended in a gurgle.

"Shoot!" commanded Grace. "Shoot high! Empty your rifle!"

Both girls let go a rattling fire with their rifles, and the howls and the shots brought the others of their party tumbling and shouting from their tents.

"Down! Quiet!" commanded Grace. "Let no one shoot without orders, unless in an emergency. I am going out there."

"Better not," advised Miss Briggs.

"I must. You know I must. If they have harmed that boy--Well, you know the answer. Keep them quiet."

With only her revolver, Grace crept around the outer edge of the camp, making every movement with extreme care, pausing now and then to listen. It was her opinion that the disturbers had left, but she was too old a campaigner to take that for granted, and never for an instant relaxed her caution.

The Overland girl reached the far end of the camp without incident. She crept to the tent where the colored boy slept and found it empty. There was no trace, that she was able to discover in the dark, to indicate what had happened to him. Not satisfied with what she had already accomplished, Grace crept further out along the trail, revolver in hand, eyes and ears keenly on the alert.

Finally she turned campwards.

"They have got the boy," she announced, coming up from the rear of the tents, and approaching her companions from behind. All were sitting on the ground, silent, expectant, waiting, either for Grace's return or a burst of revolver fire. Their nerves jumped from the reaction when Grace spoke to them.

"Oh, that is too bad," murmured Anne.

"Did you discover anything else?" asked Elfreda.

"No. I could not see anything in the dark. The worst of it is that we shall not be able to do a thing until morning. That settles our getting started in the morning, for I for one shall not leave here until we have found Washington. I don't know why they should have taken the boy. He surely can be of no use to them."

"He can give them information, can't he?" asked Hippy.

"None that will be of use to them."

"It is my opinion," spoke up Elfreda, "that they were not after the boy at all, but that his howls made it necessary for them to take him to protect themselves. Of course they will drag such information as he has, from him."

"We must all stand watch for the rest of the night," announced Hippy. He then promptly distributed his force, taking the lead in the arrangements, which Grace was now glad to have him do. Then again, she understood full well that Lieutenant Wingate himself was eager to even up old scores with the men who had handled him so roughly.

Each girl, armed with a rifle, took the position assigned to her, and there was no more conversation for the next two hours, no sound other than that from the insect life and the occasional whinney of a pony. The minds of the Overlanders, however, were active. They were pondering over these persistent attacks on them, and Grace, for one, became finally convinced that Lieutenant Wingate was not overstating when he declared that there was a price on his head. She was inclined to think, too, that the same condition applied to all members of the Overland party.

As for Washington, none of them believed that the mountaineers could have any possible motive for harming him, unless, perhaps, it were necessary to do so for their own protection. That, the girls realized, was a grave possibility, especially were the men to see that he recognized any of them.

There was worry on the minds of the Overlanders, and the hours of their vigil seemed to drag out interminably. It was not until morning, however, that anything occurred to disturb them or even rouse them from their endless listening and peering into the darkness with straining eyes and bated breaths. Therefore, the interruption that followed the long, tense silence came as a shock, an interruption that startled each member of the party into a new and throbbing alertness.

# CHAPTER XI
## "A MARKED MAN"

The first indication that something was approaching the opposite side of the camp was made known by the sudden restlessness of the ponies, which sprang up and gave every indication of fright.

The action of the ponies was followed by a floundering and crashing out there in the bushes as if a large animal were tearing its way through them.

"Hold your fire!" directed Lieutenant Wingate in a low voice. "It may be that one of the ponies has broken loose."

No one answered, but every rifle was held at ready.

"There it comes! It's a man," cried Nora, as a figure burst into view from the bushes.

"Doan shoot! Doan shoot! It am Wash," howled Washington Washington, then tripping on a vine, he fell flat on his face. "It kotched me! It kotched me!" he bellowed, springing up ready to make another dash.

By this time Hippy had him by the collar.

"Oh, fiddlesticks! All this scare for a black nightmare," groaned Emma.

"Stop that racket!" commanded Hippy. "Is any one chasing you?"

"Ah--Ah doan know. Ah--Ah reckons de debbil hisself am chasing me. Ah--"

"Pull yourself together and tell us what happened to you," directed Grace as Lieutenant Wingate led the trembling lad up to them.

"He got me, he did."

"Who got you?" interjected Miss Briggs.

"Ah doan know. He kotched me an' Ah yelled--"

"He yelled? How unusual," muttered Emma.

"Den--den he put er hand ovah ma mouth an' gib me er clip on de haid," continued Washington excitedly. "Ah doan knows nothin' moah till Ah wakes up. Dey was talkin' 'bout dat time."

"Who was talking?" interrupted Hippy.

"Dis heah niggah doan know nothin' 'bout dat. Dey was talkin', an' den Ah jest jumps up--an' den Ah jumps up an runs away."

"How did you find your way here?" asked Anne.

"That is what I have been wondering," nodded Grace.

"Ah didn'. A feller kotched me when Ah runned, an' held mah mouf shut so Ah couldn't holler. Den he-all fotched me heah. Den he gib me er kick an' says, 'Gwine on, yuh lazy niggah, but look out fer de guns. Dem folks kin shoot.' Dat's why Ah hollered when Ah kim inter de camp," finished Washington.

"Did you recognize any of the men who took you away from here?" questioned Miss Briggs.

Washington shook his curly head.

"Did you know the man who brought you back?" asked Grace.

"Ah did not. Who yuh reckons he was?"

"That is what we are trying to find out," Hippy informed him. "Would you know the man were you to see him again?"

"Ah didn' see him nohow. Ah felt him, Ah did, an' Ah feels him yit, Ah does."

"No need to question him," laughed Grace. "His militant friend was rather violent, it appears. Washington, get your blanket and lie down here near the tents. The camp is being guarded and you will be perfectly safe. The others had better turn in also, and get what rest they can. It now lacks only about two hours to daylight, and we shall be able to make an early start, now that Washington is here."

"Yes, he's here, but he would not be here if I had not con-centrated on him," spoke up Emma Dean.

"For the love of goodness, drop that piffle!" begged Hippy wearily. "We have enough serious matters on hand to think about without having to listen to prattle. Laundry, did you know that Miss Dean had been 'con-centrating' on you?"

"What dat? Er hoodoo?"

"Yes, that is what Miss Dean is trying to put on you," laughed Hippy.

"You listen to me, Wash!" demanded Emma spiritedly. "When I was con-centrating on you, making my mind reach out to yours, didn't your hair seem to stand on end just the way a cat's hair does when you stroke it the wrong way--"

"Yes'm! Mah hair stood up all right when dey kotched me," admitted Washington.

"And didn't you feel a distinct electric shock all over your being?"

"Just like as if you had run into an electric light pole?" interjected Hippy.

"No, suh. Didn' feel no shock, 'cept when dat feller kicked me. Ah felt dat all right an' Ah feels it yit."

"I reckon that will be about all. You see, Emma, this was not a case of mind over matter, but of a heavy boot against Washington Washington's anatomy," chuckled Hippy.

The Overland Riders laughed louder than their situation warranted, and Emma Dean, very red in the face, flounced off to her tent without another word.

"I think that was real mean of you, Hippy," chided Grace, laughing in spite of her effort to be stern.

Soon after that the camp settled down to quietness, with Hippy Wingate and Elfreda Briggs on guard, Grace having consented to lie down and sleep for the rest of the night--provided.

They were undisturbed, except when, shortly before daylight, something again aroused the ponies, but the disturbance quickly subsided, and the watchers believed that some animal had startled them.

At daylight the camp was astir--that is, with the exception of Hippy Wingate who insisted on a brief beauty nap after his two-hour vigil. He came out just as Washington, after building the cook-fire, was starting out to water the horses.

"Good morning, Lieutenant," greeted Emma Dean sweetly. "What's the quotation this morning?"

"On what?" demanded Hippy, halting and eyeing her suspiciously.

"On heads, of course."

"Is there any reason why, because I'm a marked man--because there is a price on my head, you should make fun of me? Having a price on one's head is not a joking matter. My mind is carrying a heavy weight, Emma Dean," rebuked Hippy impressively.

"Nonsense! I know better. If it was carrying a heavy burden your mind long ago would have caved in," retorted Emma.

Hippy Wingate threw up his hands in token of surrender, and breaking off a twig of laurel he gravely placed it in Emma's hair so that it drooped over her forehead.

"I bestow upon thee a crown of laurel," announced Hippy solemnly amid shouts of laughter.

"Come, children. Breakfast is ready," called Grace Harlowe. "Washington!"

"Ah'm comin'," answered the colored boy from the bush. "Ah found dis on de saddle," he announced, holding out an envelope to Grace.

She took it wonderingly.

"What's this? The rural free delivery man here so early in the morning!" questioned Emma.

"This is addressed to you, Lieutenant," said Grace, handing the envelope to Lieutenant Wingate.

Hippy read it and a frown grew on his face, deepening as he read it a second time.

"More mystery?" questioned Anne Nesbit.

"Yes. Listen to this, will you?"

Hippy read out loud the following words, almost illegible on the much smeared paper:

"'Yuh-all will git out o' these mountings right
smart. We-all knows who yuh be. We-all knows why
yuh be here. Turn aroun' an' git out or it'll be
th' wus fer yuh-all.'"

"They propose to drive us out, do they?" murmured Grace.

"I looked for something of the sort," nodded Elfreda. "Is the letter signed?"

"No. But wait a moment. There is a postscript here that I haven't read," said Hippy. "Talk about your mysterious forces! Just listen to this postscript, written in another hand and evidently by an intelligent person."

## CHAPTER XII
## A MOUNTAIN MYSTERY

Perhaps the postscript is to tell us that it is all a mistake and that we do not have to leave," suggested Emma.

"Listen!" commanded Hippy, then began to read:

"'Do not follow the trail you are on, on your way to Thompson's. Strike due north for half a mile and you will come up with a wagon trail, broader and safer, because you can see a long way on either side through the thin forest. Keep the broad trail for fifteen miles, take third left and second right, which will take you to Thompson's. You're all right, but be vigilant. The above warning means what it says.'"

"Is there a name signed to the postscript?" asked Miss Briggs.

Hippy shook his head.

"I know who wrote that postscript," spoke up Miss Dean. "It was our Mystery Man, Jeremiah Long."

Grace asked for the letter, which she scrutinized critically.

"No, this is not his writing," she decided.

"How do you know? He hasn't been corresponding with you," objected Hippy.

Grace explained that Mr. Long had left a note thanking the Overlanders for their hospitality. To make certain that she was right she went to her kit and fetched the note referred to, and also brought the note that had been tossed into their camp on the occasion of Hippy's disappearance. The three missives were examined by each of the Overland Riders. It was found that the message tossed into camp and the postscript of the letter found by Washington were in the same handwriting. Mr. Long's handwriting was different.

"That disposes of the theory that either of these messages was written by Mr. Long," agreed Elfreda. "The question is, who is our mysterious friend?"

"You do not think it is a trick to get us where we shall find ourselves in a tight place?" suggested Anne questioningly.

"No. I do not feel that there is a shadow of doubt that these two notes are what they appear to be--the suggestions of a friend. Who or what he is we may or may not learn. I propose that we follow the advice he gives us. Are you all agreed on that?" asked Grace.

The Overlanders said they were.

"Then we will go on our way," directed Grace.

They found the wagon trail after nearly an hour's hard riding over rocks, into and out of gullies with steep, precipitous sides, but the wagon trail when reached, while rutty, was so much better that they soon forgot the discomforts of riding "across lots," as Hippy put it.

The noon halt was a brief one, after which they pressed on, having no difficulty in finding their way as directed by their mysterious adviser.

It was nearly dark when they came in sight of a clearing of several acres covered with growing corn, which they surmised to be part of the Thompson farm. Grace asked Washington if it were.

"Ah reckons it be," answered the colored boy, but it was apparent that he knew no more about it than did the Overland Riders.

"Where is the house of this Thompson party?" demanded Hippy.

"Mebby 'bout er whoop an' er holler from heah."

"Huh!" grunted Hippy. "The last 'whoop and holler' you told us of was nearly twenty miles. Don't guess. If you don't know the correct answer to a question, say so. Don't stall around and--"

"Yassuh."

"I suppose we should ask permission before we camp on private property," suggested Elfreda. "Not knowing where to do so, might it not be wise to back up a little?"

"What do you mean?" asked Grace.

"Move away from the trail and into the thicket where we shall be both out of sight and probably on no man's land, as it were."

"The suggestion is good, though I do not wholly approve of the idea of getting into a pocket where we cannot see about us," agreed Grace. "Our mysterious friend must know what he is talking about when he advises us to go to Thompson's farm, as some one urged Hippy to do."

"He seemed to think we would be safer here," nodded Lieutenant Wingate.

"So far as my observation goes--has gone for the last couple of years--safety is not the one great ambition of our young lives. At least, getting into difficulties and perilous situations has become a habit with Grace Harlowe," declared Miss Briggs.

"Yes, for instance, roping bandits with that Mexican lasso that the cowboys gave her last season," suggested Emma. "Why aren't you throwing it more? I have seen you swing it only once since we started."

Grace said that she had practiced with the rope nearly all winter, and declared that it was about time that the rest of the party took up throwing the lasso. Elfreda, as related in a previous volume, "GRACE HARLOWE'S OVERLAND RIDERS ON THE GREAT AMERICAN DESERT," also had learned to throw the lasso and could do so quite well, but since her winter's practice with it Grace had gained much skill and was far ahead of her friend in its manipulation. Perhaps, having mastered the secret of rope-throwing, she had lost interest in it.

"I will start practicing again to-morrow," promised Miss Briggs.

"You need it. I don't believe you could even catch cold with a rope," teased Lieutenant Wingate.

"Yes I could--I--" Elfreda's following remark was lost in the laughter of her companions. "What I said, but which you folks were too impolite to listen to, was that I will show you whether I can throw a rope or not. Let me have it, Grace."

"You will find it just inside of my tent, on the left-hand side. What are you going to do?"

"I am going out, as soon as it is light enough to see, and practice until breakfast time."

This Miss Briggs did with the graying of the dawn, after a night of peaceful rest, while Grace and Hippy kept guard over the camp. They teased her at breakfast, and Hippy suggested that Elfreda ask Emma Dean to "con-centrate" on her during Miss Briggs' future practice with the lasso.

"To change the subject, I am going to look up the Thompsons and try to make peace with them, provided they are like most of the mountaineers that we have come into intimate contact with," announced Grace. "I suggest that you and I ride out on a tour of investigation this morning, leaving Hippy here to protect the camp, Elfreda. You may take your rope along and practice on me, if you wish," smiled Grace.

"You will be perfectly safe," murmured Emma.

Immediately after breakfast the two girls mounted and rode out along the trail they had been following, now bordered on one side by a field of rustling corn. Reaching the end of the cornfield they discovered, just ahead, a cabin located in an open space of several acres of rugged mountain land.

"That must be the place. We will ride up and find out," announced Grace, clucking to her pony.

As they approached the cabin a slovenly looking woman, accompanied by three children, one a girl that the Overlanders judged to be about fourteen years of age, the other two girls being much younger, one a mere toddler, came out and, shading her eyes with a hand, eyed the newcomers suspiciously.

"Is this Mr. Thompson's home?" asked Grace, smiling down at the children.

"Ah reckon it be. Who be you?"

"I am Mrs. Grace Gray. My companion is Miss Briggs. We are riding through the mountains for pleasure and business combined, and are camped with our party on the other side of the cornfield. What I wished to ask, if you are Mrs. Thompson, is, may we be permitted to remain there for a few days?"

"Ah reckon ye kin if ye wants to if mah husband ain't objectin'."

"Is he here?" interjected Elfreda.

The woman shook her head.

"Mah other daughter is out pickin' berries. Mebby she'll come down an' look ye over bymeby. Kin I sell ye anything!"

"Yes, if you have milk we should be glad to have some every morning and night while here. We have a man friend and a colored boy with us. One of them will call for the milk early this evening. Thank you so much. Are the children quite well?"

"Tol'bly, tol'bly, Ah reckon."

"I think we have a little candy left. I will send it over to them later," said Grace smilingly, as she wheeled her pony and trotted back towards camp.

"What a sight! Think of living as those people do," reflected Elfreda.

"Perhaps they are just as happy as we are. But those poor puny children! I am sorry for them, and when I think of my daughter, Yvonne, and that healthy young animal, Lindy, your adopted daughter, I feel like crying."

"Don't! Your eyes do not look nice when, they are red. By the way, those two kiddies, despite what the mother says, do not look at all well. Did you observe how red their faces were and how listless they appeared?"

Grace said she did. She wondered, too, what the other daughter was like. Her wonder in this direction was gratified before she had been back from her brief journey twenty minutes. While telling their companions of the mountaineer's wife and family and the appearance of the woman and children, a figure rose up from behind a bush and stood curiously regarding the Overland party.

Washington discovered the newcomer and began to chatter and point.

"Don't shoot. It's a woman," cried Emma.

"No one is going to shoot," retorted Hippy hopelessly.

By this time all the girls were on their feet, gazing at the head and shoulders of a young woman showing above the bush. Her full cheeks and lips were red, and the black, straight hair hanging down her back reminded the Overlanders of Indian squaws they had seen in their journey over the Old Apache Trail. It was the caller's eyes, however, that attracted the most attention. They were large, black and full, and one felt that they were capable of blazing.

"Won't you come in, Miss?" urged Miss Briggs. "May I ask your name?" she added, as the girl, whom she judged was not much past twenty years of age, stepped out into the open.

"Ah'm Julie." That was the only information vouchsafed by the caller, and the only words she spoke for nearly the entire half hour of her stay. The Overland girls plied her with questions, and by a nod in answer to their question learned that Julie was the daughter of the woman they had called on shortly before. They called her by her first name, though now and then Emma would address her as "Miss Thompson," which seemed to perplex Julie.

"My Paw mebby'll drive ye folks off. He don't like no strangers in these parts," she finally jerked out.

"It will not be necessary. We shall be moving on in a few days," replied Grace.

"Paw don't want no strangers," insisted the girl stubbornly. "Spec'ly since he had er gun fight with one o' them. My gosh how them bullets did fly. Paw got one through his stumik and had er right smart trouble with his eatin' fer two days arter that. What you-all doin'?" she demanded, eyeing Nora Wingate, who was making a sweater.

"Crocheting, Julie. Knitting, perhaps you call it."

"Uh-huh. My gran'ma kin beat you-all knittin'."

"Yes?" smiled Nora.

"You bet she kin. Why, whad you-all think? Gran'ma takes her knittin' ter bed with 'er and every now and then she throws out a sock. I'll bet a cookie you-all kain't knit like that-away."

"You win," chuckled Hippy, and the Overland girls laughed merrily.

"I'm going now. Maw said as I'd better come down and look you-all over, cause Paw'll want ter know 'bout you-all. Say! Goin' to the dance?"

"When?" questioned Emma, her interest instantly aroused.

"Sat'dy night to the schoolhouse over in the holler yonder. Mebby you-all kin help we uns to pay the band."

"What? Do you have a band up here?" wondered Anne.

"Uh-huh--fiddle and er banjer, and the feller that plays the banjer kin tear more music out o' it and stomp on the floor harder'n any other perfesser in the mountains. Better come if Paw ain't run you-all out befo' then."

"Don't worry, little one. Paw won't run this outfit out just yet," replied Hippy.

"I dunno, I dunno. Ain't no tellin' 'bout Paw. Bye." Julie pushed a mass of hair from her forehead, gave her head a jerk to settle the hair more firmly in place, then, turning on her heel, walked away without once turning her head.

"With a stomach like his, 'Paw' should have been in France fighting the Boches," observed Emma Dean solemnly. "I'm going to the dance! I'm going to the dance! Tra-la-la," she cried, doing a fancy step about the camp, keeping time with her upraised arms until she stepped on Washington Washington's foot and brought a howl from that worthy.

The Overland girls then fell upon and subdued Miss Dean without loss of time.

"If you let her go to that dance there will be a riot, as sure as I am a foot high," declared Hippy Wingate, in which assertion most of the girls agreed with him.

## CHAPTER XIII
## THREE MEN IN THE CORNFIELD

Ah tells yuh, Ah did. Ah sawed him obah dar in de co'nfield," protested Washington Washington.

"There you go again. You will saw the wrong person one of these days, then you will go to jail for life," rebuked Emma Dean.

"What's that?" demanded Grace, hurrying to the excited colored boy, who was rolling his eyes and gesticulating as he tried to tell the Overlanders what he had seen.

"Laundry performed a surgical operation on a man in the cornfield. That's all, Grace," Emma Dean informed her.

"Ah did. Ah sawed his gun, too."

"Yours must be a sharp saw if it will saw a gun," murmured Emma.

"He war peekin' at yuh-all, an' when he seed Ah sawed him he snooked an' Ah didn't sawed him no moah."

"Is that all?" questioned Grace.

"Yassuh. Yes'm."

"Quite likely it was the man who owns the cornfield. He probably was looking the crop over to see if it were fit to cut. I presume a man has a perfect right to look at his own cornfield, even up here in the Kentucky mountains," observed Miss Briggs.

"Ah reckons you're right," chuckled Hippy. "I decline to get excited over it. I have troubles of my own. Say!" he added, his face growing suddenly serious. "You don't suppose it was a fellow trying to collect that head money on me, do you?"

"Not in broad daylight, Hippy," smiled Grace. "The headsman probably will perform the delicate operation of decapitating you some night when you are asleep."

"Nonsense!" exclaimed Nora. "The mountain air has made you all light-headed. I know who it was. It was 'Paw.' Paw has returned and was looking us over. I hope, for our own peace of mind, that he liked our looks."

"Nora may be right," nodded Anne.

"Yes," agreed Grace. "I think it would be wise for Hippy to go to the Thompson home for the milk to-night. He can then get acquainted with Mr. Thompson, and perhaps interest him, and make him friendly to us."

Hippy eyed her disapprovingly and sighed.

"A lamb was led to the slaughter and--"

"Just the same, we must be alert to-night," advised Grace. "If Hippy and Elfreda will take the first half of the night, Anne and I will take the watch the balance of the night."

This was agreed to, and the rest of the day was devoted to setting the camp to rights, practicing with the rope, at which all tried their hand, and taking naps, always with attention to their surroundings, for the Overland Riders knew they were in more or less peril in the Kentucky mountains, and believed that sooner or later those who, for some reason, wished to be rid of them, would make a desperate attempt to force them to leave that neighborhood.

There was the warning note to indicate that the attempt might not be long delayed.

Supper, that evening, was eaten just after dark, as the Overlanders enjoyed sitting about their campfire in the cool evening air, chatting and telling stories and indulging in good-natured banter as they ate. They had just sat down when a voice from the darkness brought instant silence, and a quick reaching for their weapons. The nerves of the Overland girls were getting jumpy.

"I make the near-blind to see and the seeing to see better. I am the promoter of happiness, the benefactor of all-uns of the mountains. Specs, ladies and gentlemen. Nick-nacks, thread, needles, but principally specs and good cheer. Yes, thanks. I will have a snack with you. I thank you for the invitation."

The Overland Riders, who, up to this juncture, had not uttered a word, burst into laughter, for they recognized that voice, the never-to-be-forgotten voice and lingo of Jeremiah Long, the Mystery Man.

"You are indeed welcome," greeted Grace, stepping forward to shake hands with the spectacle man, who put down his grip, mopped his forehead, then grasped her hand, regarding Grace with twinkling eyes.

"I have just come from Jed Thompson's hospitable home where I have spectacled the family from the old man himself down to and including the babe. They told me that down by the cornfield was a bunch of campers, and I said I'd go down and sell them some specs. I'll introduce myself. I don't know you," he added in a lower tone. "I'm Jeremiah Long, and I've already told you the rest. Who are you?"

"We are the Overland Riders, riding through the mountains for pleasure--and business," answered Grace, quickly catching his intimation that he did not desire that listening ears should know that he had met the party before. "After mess you must show us your wares. Perhaps we may find something that may be useful to us."

"Charmed, I'm sure." The Mystery Man of the mountains placed a hand over his heart and made a profound bow. He then sat down. "Cream and sugar in the coffee, please. Thank you. I caught the odor of this coffee before I rounded the upper corner of the cornfield. My nose frequently leads me to the good things of earth, and what I don't then see with my own eyes, the eyes in my case do."

"I would give almost anything to be able to talk a blue streak the way you do," exclaimed Emma so earnestly that her companions nearly choked with laughter, and that left the Mystery Man with laughter instead of words on his lips.

"Yes, but greater even than the gift of gab, is the gift of 'con-centration,'" twinkled Jeremiah Long.

"How did you know about that?" demanded Emma, looking her amazement.

"How did I know? My dear young woman, the essence sent out by 'con-centration' is an imponderable quantity--"

"Imponderable?" wondered Miss Dean. "I like that word, and, though I don't know what it means, it sounds good."

"As I was saying, the waves sent out by your 'con-centrating' may have, like the wireless waves, been picked up by my own delicate mental mechanism and--"

"In other words, Miss Dean overshot the mark she aimed at," interjected Hippy.

"Well, something like that, I should say," chuckled the Mystery Man.

"Is there anything you do not know?" wondered Anne Nesbit.

"You are a mighty fortunate man, I should say," declared Hippy. "Think what the result would have been had that 'imponderable quantity' hit you fair and square. Why, it would have blown you to atoms--molecules and--"

"Suppose we change the subject," suggested Grace Harlowe. "Show us your wares, won't you, Mr. Long?"

The visitor got up, and, fetching his case, opened it, revealing great numbers of shining spectacles, beads and other shoddy adornments.

"We will now fit you to glasses, those of you who need them."

"You, of course, know how to examine eyes?" nodded Elfreda.

"Oh, no. I 'fit' the bows to the ears," answered Mr. Long.

"Yes, but aren't you afraid you will ruin the eyes of the persons you fit glasses to?" questioned Grace.

The Mystery Man smiled.

"I never heard of a person's eyes being ruined by looking through a window," he made reply, raising a merry laugh. "I'll fit you to smoked glasses to protect your eyes from the sun. They won't cost you anything. Neither did they cost me anything. I want my wares known in every home in the mountains, and I want every man, woman and child, and babe in arms, to be seeing things through my eyes, and I'll accomplish it if the window glass holds out."

"Of course we expect to pay you," began Grace.

"Not a cent, not a cent. I should say it might be wise to have them--the glasses--well smoked up like a ham, for there may be doings up here that it were the part of wisdom for you folks not to see. Do the bows fit, Mrs. Gray?" he asked, adjusting a pair of specs to her ears.

"I--I think so."

The visitor rattled on, keeping his customers fairly convulsed with laughter, until he had equipped half the party with spectacles.

"You may pay me," he suddenly suggested, lowering his voice. "I've changed my mind. That will be two dollars apiece," he added in a loud, blustering tone.

The Overland Riders looked at him in amazement. Only a few moments before that he had proposed to "fit" them with glasses free of charge.

"Of course we will pay you," announced Emma Dean airily.

Elfreda and Grace, who had been eyeing Mr. Long inquiringly, saw motive in his sudden change. The quick, meaning glance he gave them convinced them that their surmise was right.

"What is it?" asked Grace, her voice down almost to a whisper.

"Yes, two dollars. Thank you. There are three men in the cornfield watching us," he added in a tone barely loud enough for the Overlanders to hear. "Don't look. If I don't run out of change I'll have you all fixed up in three shakes of a possum's tail," said Mr. Long, again boisterously.

## CHAPTER XIV
## ELFREDA DISTINGUISHES HERSELF

The smoke is too thick. I can't see through the glasses. I want my money back," complained Emma.

"No extra charge for the additional soot. Who is next? Ah! Wash needs a pair of specs to tone down the whites of his eyes," cried Jeremiah.

"Never mind him. He is smoky enough as it is," returned Hippy. "If you are dead set on doing more business you might go out and put goggles on the mules. Perhaps then they might not see so much to bray at."

This badinage was kept up for some little time, so that the prowlers in the cornfield might not suspect that their presence were known to the campers.

All of the party were wondering how the Mystery Man knew that they were being watched, for none of the Overlanders had heard the slightest sound in the direction of the cornfield, and their ears, after all their campaigning, were always on the alert. Jeremiah was a man of many mysteries.

Grace invited him to share their hospitality for the night, which he acknowledged by rising and favoring them with another profound bow.

"I will sleep in the open, if I may be permitted to do so--as before," he murmured. In the same low tone, he added: "I don't just like the location of your camp."

"Why not, sir?" asked Miss Briggs.

"Too many ears in the cornfield, and besides--"

Emma Dean uttered a dismal groan. Her companions burst out laughing, Jeremiah regarding them with eyes that twinkled and laughed, though the face remained almost expressionless.

"Is it not true?" he asked.

"Yes. Too true! Alas, too true," murmured Hippy in an awed tone.

Grace got up laughing and went to her tent for blankets for her guest.

"By the fire as before?" she asked upon her return.

Jeremiah shook his head.

"I will place them, Mrs. Gray. Thank you."

The girls then bade their guest good-night, each one shaking hands with him, and, as Grace extended her hand, he placed in it a roll of money.

"The funds I held you folks up for," explained Mr. Long. "You can return it to them to-morrow with an explanation. Do not let the lieutenant take too many chances, is my suggestion. Good-night."

It had been decided that, so long as their guest were to sleep in the open, it would not be necessary to keep guard outside. Grace said, however, that she would stand watch in her tent part of the night, then call Elfreda, and turn in.

Mr. Long made up his bed on the cornfield side of the camp and, after listening to one of Hippy's war stories, rolled up in his blankets and went to sleep. Grace, from her tent, could faintly make out the form of the Mystery Man, and, sitting, chin in hand regarding him, she wondered, as she had done many times before, who and what the man was. That he was all he would have them believe she did not for a moment credit.

"What's that?" Grace leaned forward and peered. Mr. Long appeared to be asleep under his blankets, but, a short distance from him, she saw another figure cautiously rolling slowly towards the cornfield.

Looking more closely at the blankets, the Overland girl saw that they were folded lengthwise to make them appear something like the form of a human being, and that it was Jeremiah himself who was so cautiously rolling away.

After waiting another hour for his return she decided that their guest had left them for the night. Grace then awakened Elfreda and asked her to take the watch for a couple of hours, saying she was very tired.

Elfreda got up sleepily and, for several minutes, sat with hands clasped to her head.

"Anything stirring?" she asked, yawning.

"Nothing except the Mystery Man. He stirred himself out of camp. He rolled out. I do not believe he will return to-night."

"Queer chap, that. All right, Loyalheart. I am awake now. Tumble in and I will see if I can keep you out of trouble until daylight."

"See to it that, instead, you don't get us into a peck of it," chuckled Grace, tucking herself in under the blankets. "Thank you for getting the bed so nice and comfy for me."

"Don't tantalize me. I know how sweet that bed is, for I just got out of it myself," replied Miss Briggs sourly. Grace did not hear, for she already was sound asleep, and Elfreda, muttering to herself, straightened up and exercised her arms and shoulders more thoroughly to arouse her sleepy faculties.

"There! I think I can manage to keep awake now. I hear Hippy snoring. Gracious! If I had a snore like that I think I should file it. Oh!"

Elfreda had seen a movement on the cornfield side of the camp. To her, it looked like a man crawling into camp.

Miss Briggs reached for her rifle and waited. Now and then little ribbons of flame flickered over the bed of coal of the campfire, lighting up the camp momentarily. Elfreda was unafraid for the weapon in her hands gave her confidence, and the cool touch of the barrel against her hand steadied it.

The intruder was now coming directly towards her.

The moving object was directly in line with Washington Washington's tent, and for that reason Miss Briggs would not have dared to fire, even did she find it necessary to do so.

Her first impulse was to awaken Grace, but upon second thought she decided to wait. Perhaps it was the Mystery Man returning, though Elfreda did not believe he would take the chance of getting shot.

"Mercy! It's an animal," gasped the watcher. "A bear!" she added in an awed whisper, as a faint mountain breeze fanned the campfire into a flame.

The bear by this time had sniffed its way across the camp, bearing to the left as it neared her tent, but halting when it reached the pack that contained their provisions. Here the animal was quite clearly outlined in the light cast by the fire.

It was a small bear, but it looked very large to Elfreda Briggs, who had never experienced meeting a bear at such close range. He began clawing at the pack of provisions and tearing with his teeth at the tough canvas covering, and had it open before Elfreda realized what he was up to.

"He is eating up our food!" she exclaimed under her breath. Miss Briggs raised her rifle to fire. She lowered it ever so little as a new thought occurred to her.

"I'll do it!" she declared, laying the rifle on the ground beside her. "I probably shall make an awful mess of the attempt, but I am going to try to rope that beast. I don't believe he will attack me if I miss. If he does I shall have every incentive to break all running records in my sprint for the rifle."

Elfreda reached for Grace Harlowe's Mexican lasso, arranged it for casting, then, after listening briefly to Grace's breathing, stepped cautiously from the tent.

The bear was tearing at the food and its covering, and grunting with satisfaction, and the supplies of the Overland Riders were disappearing at a rate that promised a famine, if Bruin's operations were not immediately checked. So busy was he that her cautious footsteps were unheard, and so deep was his snout plunged into the treasure he had found that he failed to catch the scent of his enemy.

As she neared him Miss Briggs felt a sudden weakness in the knees that threatened flight on her part, but, by summoning all her will, she managed to call back her grit.

"Ill do it if it kills me!" muttered the Overland Rider. "If I win, I shall have the laugh on Grace Harlowe. If I lose--well we won't think about that. Here goes. Steady, and 'con-centrate,' Elfreda Briggs!"

Miss Briggs swung the rope above her head three times to open the loop, and, gauging her distance as well as she knew how, she let go. One side of the loop hit Bruin on the ear.

Uttering a snarl at the interruption, the animal made a leap and accomplished what the roper had failed to accomplish. He leaped right into the loop with his head and one leg. His spring drew the lasso tightly about him. He was fast, but he did not propose to be so for many seconds. Throwing himself on his back, the bear began clawing and biting at the hateful thing that was drawing tighter and tighter about him.

Elfreda, triumphant, now highly excited, determined to hold fast to that which she had, twisted the free end of the rope about her arm and grasped the tautened strand with both hands, at the same time bracing her feet and pulling with all her might.

Bruin bounded to his feet, and for one terrible instant J. Elfreda thought he was going to rush her. Instead, the bear whirled and, humping himself almost into a furry ball, galloped away. His captor, with the rope twisted about her arm, could not have freed herself in time, even had she thought of so doing.

"Help! Oh, help!" she wailed, as her feet were jerked from under her and she was hurled violently to the ground. "Help--p!"

The camp of the Overland Riders was in an uproar in an instant. J. Elfreda, champion of peace, though not a pacifist, had started something, the end of which was not yet in sight.

## CHAPTER XV
## WHEN EMMA SAID TOO MUCH

"Where is he?" bellowed Hippy, charging from his tent, rifle in hand. "Elfreda!" shouted Grace, rubbing her eyes to get the sleep out of them. She could hear the commotion, but was unable to make out the cause of the disturbance.

In the meantime, Miss Briggs was being dragged over the ground at a rate of speed that was neither good for her clothing nor her body. In his blind fright, the animal charged straight into Washington Washington's pup-tent, landing right on the colored boy. The lad threw up his arms, and they closed about the neck of the bear.

A frightful howl instantly woke the mountain silence, as Washington let go and rolled from under. The bear, as much frightened as was Wash, turned and charged across the camp. He met Emma Dean head on, and she went down under the onslaught.

"It's a bear! Shoot him!" screamed Emma.

"No!" shouted Grace. "He is dragging Elfreda. Don't shoot!" Grace's eyes by this time had become adjusted to the uncertain light and her mind instantly comprehended the situation, so far as the fact that her companion was being dragged was concerned, though she did not realize that it was her rope that was around the neck of the frightened animal.

Young Bruin went through Grace's tent, Elfreda following him like a projectile. Both emerged from the ruins on the other side and headed for the bush, with the Overland Riders in full pursuit.

"Throw yourself on the rope and grab it!" panted Grace, as Hippy ran past her.

"Let go!" he shouted to Miss Briggs, but, though Elfreda was willing to do so, she could not. Neither could she summon enough breath to answer.

"Snub the rope around something," urged Grace.

Hippy reached and passed Elfreda and threw himself on the rope, as he thought. The bear, having made a sudden turn to get away from him, caused Hippy to miss the rope by a few feet. The rope tripped Grace who landed flat on the ground.

It was at this juncture that Anne and Nora reached the scene, and the next instant they too were tripped by the rope. The entire Overland party were now floundering about in the bushes, and Washington Washington was up a tree, clinging to it, wide-eyed, as he listened to the uproar below him.

Darting this way and that, the bear finally raced around a tree with Miss Briggs following. The purchase thus given to her served to check the progress of the animal. Hippy took instant advantage. He threw himself on the rope, and, this time, succeeded in grasping it with both hands.

"Quick! Get her loose," he panted, holding to the lasso with all his strength, but feeling it slowly slipping through his hands, for the bear possessed greater pulling strength than did Hippy.

Grace lost no time in freeing the rope from Elfreda's hands and arm.

"Drag her away. Lively!" she urged.

Anne and Nora gave instant obedience, and the instant Elfreda was free of the rope, Grace quickly snubbed it about the trunk of the tree.

"Let go, Hippy," she called. "I think I can hold him till you get here to help me."

Bruin was snarling and plunging, throwing himself this way and that in his vain efforts to free himself, but the hair rope held. Mere bear strength was not equal to breaking a woven hair rope, and, when Hippy threw his weight on the end of it with Grace, they hauled the animal up towards the tree little by little, Bruin fighting every inch of the way.

"Watch him," warned the lieutenant.

As he neared the tree, the animal showed fight but Grace and Hippy made the rope fast when the bear was a yard or so from the tree, fearing to draw him any closer to themselves.

"How is Elfreda?" called Grace, fanning herself with her hat.

"Sadly mussed," answered Nora.

"Well, now that you have him, what do you propose to do with him?" demanded Grace, walking over and gazing down at Miss Briggs, who lay on the ground breathing hard.

"I--I have done all I ca--an," groaned Elfreda.

"I should say you had. What happened, Elfreda?"

"Mostly myself. You ought to know that by looking at me." Miss Briggs' face was scratched from contact with the bushes; her hair was down and in a tangle, and her clothing was torn. She was a much mussed-up young woman.

"Watch him, Hippy," called Grace. "J. Elfreda, if you are feeling able please tell us what occurred. I know that you roped the animal, but that is all."

Miss Briggs briefly related her experience up to the time the Overlanders appeared on the scene.

"You win the blue ribbon," laughed Grace. "As I asked before, now that you have the beast, what do you propose to do with him?"

"Let him go," replied Elfreda a little petulantly.

"Yes, but how? You roped him. It seems up to you to untie him."

"Oh, cut the rope," suggested Emma.

"Indeed, you will not," objected Grace. "You must think of some better plan."

"Leave it to the bear. He will have the rope gnawed in two very soon at the present rate," called Hippy. "Come, Emma. Get busy and 'con-centrate' on the difficulty."

The animal was on its back when the girls gathered about him, keeping a safe distance from him, however. He was clawing and biting and snarling savagely, and Grace was much concerned for her rope, which was one of her prized possessions.

"What do you suggest, Hippy?" she asked.

"Either cut the rope or shoot him, or else let him liberate himself."

"He will have to be shot. I am sorry, but it seems the only way," decided Grace. "Will you do it, Hippy?"

"Sure I will. Mighty glad for the opportunity. We will have bear steak for breakfast."

"Perhaps we shall have jail to digest it in. I am not certain whether or not we are permitted to shoot bear at this time of the year. Do you know what the Kentucky game laws with reference to bear are?"

Hippy said he did not, and did not care. Having made up his mind to have bear for breakfast, no mere laws should interfere with his appetite he said. The girls, not wishing to witness the operation, returned to the camp and Hippy shot the bear.

Most of the balance of the night was spent by him in dressing the animal and stringing it up by its hocks to let it cool. He was not an expert at this sort of thing, but had Tom Gray been there he would have done the job and been back between his blankets in an hour. However, there was bear steak for breakfast, though Elfreda declared she wouldn't touch a mouthful of it for anything. The others were not suffering from delicate appetites, and did full justice to the meal.

Later in the forenoon, Hippy, who had declared himself too busy to go for the milk the night before, started out for the Thompson cabin, accompanied by Nora and Emma, to purchase a pail of fresh milk.

Upon their arrival there, Julie and the rest of the family, except Mr. Thompson, gathered about the Overland Riders, full of curiosity. Julie explained that "Paw" had gone away the night before and hadn't come back.

"Paw's awful mad 'bout you folks," she announced. "Said as how ye had better git out afore he got too het up 'bout ye."

"We shall be going in a few days," answered Nora. "Tell your 'Paw' not to get excited."

"I'll tell you what," bubbled Emma. "Does he like bear meat?"

"Ah reckon he likes most any kind o' food," answered Mrs. Thompson.

"Good. Listen to me! We got a bear last night and we had part of him for breakfast. For a time it looked like he was going to have us for his breakfast, but we shot him and Lieutenant Wingate dressed him, and he was fine," declared Miss Dean with enthusiasm. "I will send the colored boy over with a fine bear steak for Mr. Thompson, and, if he is anything like Lieutenant Wingate, he will be mad no longer."

The mountain woman smiled at Emma's temperamental enthusiasm.

"I reckon he'll be mighty glad to have it," she nodded.

Before leaving, Hippy Wingate chucked the two little children under the chin and gave each a five-cent piece, promising to give them as much more each time he came for the milk.

"Queer about 'Paw,' ain't it?" mimicked Emma as they were on their way home. "I wonder if he is staying in the cornfield watching our camp. Perhaps he'll come out when he hears there is bear steak at home. My, but aren't those children dirty?"

Grace frowned when Nora told her of Emma's offer to give the Thompsons some of the bear meat.

"Emma, no good ever comes from babbling. I am sorry you did that, but so long as you promised you must make good," directed Grace.

"All right. Don't be so frightfully touchy. I will send Wash over with a hind leg."

"No. You will send or take a steak, as you promised. A bear's leg! The idea!"

"I don't know what you mean. A leg of lamb is considered a real delicacy where I come from, and I should think a leg of bear would be an equally delightful delicacy up here where the beast grows."

Even Miss Briggs joined in the laugh that followed, though it hurt frightfully to exercise her facial muscles.

Hippy said he would cut out a steak, but Nora decided that he must have assistance or he would be sending something that not even the mountaineers could eat. A black chunk of meat that weighed all of twelve pounds was the result of the carving. This Hippy tied up in a roll and gave to Washington to take to the Thompsons.

"Our peace offering to 'Paw,'" observed Hippy as the colored boy, with the bear meat on his shoulder, trudged away playing his harmonica. "That dance that Julie invited us to attend, comes off to-morrow night. She asked me to-day, if we were going. I said I reckoned we'd be over, and asked her if she would trip the light fantastic with me, but Julie shook her head. What about it? Do we go or stay?"

"What will we do about the camp?" wondered Grace.

"Leave it here, of course," urged Emma.

"And find it missing when we return," suggested Elfreda. "I fear that won't do at all."

"We can hide our equipment and ride the ponies over to Coon Hollow, with Laundry along on one of the mules to look after our horses when we get there," planned Lieutenant Wingate.

"What about the other mule?" questioned Anne.

"Let him take care of himself. If any stranger attempts to fool around that mule he will get the everlasting daylights kicked out of him. Nora, you had better shake your feet up to-day and get in practice, for to-morrow night you dance--if--"

"Yes, if," laughed Grace. "It shall be just as you people wish. Personally I am not keen for it, except that it will be a treat to watch the mountain folk at play."

All except Miss Briggs were enthusiastic for the dance.

"With my damaged countenance, I shan't be able to dance," she complained.

"You don't intend to dance on your face, do you!" wondered Emma.

"If I perform the way I did with the bear, I undoubtedly shall. There is no telling what I might do."

"You ought to have a net to perform over, like the circus people do," declared Emma. "Do we go?"

"Yes, let's go," urged Nora.

The others being of the same mind, Grace gave a rather reluctant consent and the matter was settled then and there, greatly adding to the happiness of Emma Dean.

That afternoon Grace made an inspection of the cornfield and discovered the imprints of heavy boots in the soft dirt near the camp. There had been, she believed, four men in the party, and all four evidently had been spying on the Overland camp. She followed their trail until she came to the edge of the cornfield, facing the Thompson cabin. Grace shrugged her shoulders and retraced her steps.

"I have a feeling that our affairs must come to a head soon," she murmured. "The footprints, after leaving the cornfield, appear to lead directly towards the Thompson home. However, we shall see. The night may bring something in the way of a development. I am getting tired of the waiting policy. Girls," called Grace, as she entered the camp. "What do you say if we break camp and get out to-morrow?"

"You forget the dance," reminded Emma, who did not propose to miss such an opportunity as this.

"Day after to-morrow, then?" questioned Grace.

"In spite of warnings and the suggestion of our unseen friend?" asked Anne.

"Yes. We can't stay here forever. Besides, the days are passing and we have some little distance to go before reaching the rendezvous where we are to meet

Tom. What we need is action."

"Did I not start something for you last night? What more do you want?" demanded Miss Briggs.

"To keep moving. You started the wrong way. You were headed towards home when you set out behind your bear," laughed Grace. "What do you say, girls?"

"Yes. Let's go," nodded Elfreda. "Nothing much matters after last night, so far as I am concerned." The rest left the decision entirely in Grace Harlowe's hands, and she decided to move as suggested, provided nothing intervened to prevent their doing so.

Bear meat, coffee with real cream and fresh vegetables, procured from the Thompsons, made an unusually appetizing supper that night, and during the meal Washington furnished music to entertain them. He was still playing when Anne warned her companions that a man had just stepped out of the cornfield and was coming into camp.

The Overlanders got up, wondering who their caller might be.

"Evenin', folks," greeted the stranger, who was of the same gaunt, razor-faced type that they had come in contact with on other occasions on this journey.

"Good evening," answered the Overland Riders pleasantly.

"We have just finished supper, but won't you sit down and have a snack?" asked Grace. "There is some meat and coffee left."

"Reckon Ah will, thankee."

The caller sat down, tucked his red handkerchief under his chin, hitched his revolver holster back a little further, leaned over and sniffed at his heaping plate of bear meat, then fell to with a will. "He ate as if he had had nothing to eat for a fortnight," as Emma confided to Anne Nesbit. Washington made a fresh pot of coffee for him.

"Reckon this 'ere's as fine a piece o' beef as Ah ever stowed," observed the guest, rolling his eyes up to the assembled Riders.

"It isn't beef. It's--" began Emma, but quickly subsided as Anne pinched her warningly.

"It's what?" demanded the caller.

"Codfish!" answered Emma lamely.

The stranger shrugged his shoulders and resumed his eating.

"Ahem!" said Hippy by way of clearing his throat. "It is a fine, large evening. Do you ordinarily have such large evenings in the Kentucky mountains?"

"Off an' on, Mister. Wall, Ah reckon Ah'm full clear to the gullet. Who be ye-all?"

"We call ourselves the Overland Riders. May I ask who you are?" questioned Hippy.

"Ah'm the game constable of this 'ere county. Where's the bear?"

"Some--some of it is--is inside of you," gasped Emma Dean a little hysterically.

## CHAPTER XVI
## A JOKE ON THE OVERLANDERS

H elp!" murmured Elfreda Briggs.

"The game constable!" repeated Lieutenant Wingate. "Oh! Glad to know you, old man. Glad to know you. This is a genuine pleasure, I assure you. How is business? Are you arresting any game--rabbits, possums, or anything of that sort?" went on Hippy jovially, to hide his real feelings.

Grace Harlowe laughed in a low tone.

"Ah may be. Ah asked, where is the bear?"

"Bear, bear?" questioned the lieutenant, glancing about him inquiringly. "I--I didn't know that you had lost one. What sort of a looking bear was he, and did he wear a license tag on his collar or--"

"Oh, shet up!" growled the constable. "That was bear meat Ah had fer mah supper. No one ain't allowed to have bear meat till December."

"Then why did you eat what you say was bear meat?" demanded Miss Briggs in her severest legal tone. "You say no one is allowed to have bear meat until December, but it appears to me that you have had your share of it this evening."

"Whut's that over thar?" he exploded, pointing to where the carcass of Elfreda's bear was faintly discernible, hanging by its hocks from a pole suspended between two trees. The constable strode over and peered at what was left of Mr. Bruin.

"So, that's what yer up to in these 'ere mountings, eh?"

Hippy shrugged his shoulders.

"You win," he said. "What is the answer?"

"Wall, Ah reckons as if you'd pay me fer the bear an'--an' settle fer the damages, Ah might--"

"Settle nothing!" roared Hippy in a tone calculated to frighten the visitor, but which failed to have that effect. "Why, I could have you arrested for trying to accept a bribe from a former United States officer. You will get no bribe from me."

"Ah'll arrest the whole pack of ye. Officer, eh? Ah reckoned as ye was that. Ah did, an' seein' as ye admit it, ain't nothin' more to be said 'bout that, but Ah'll take ye in and clap ye in the calaboose jest the same. Yer under arrest! All of ye is under arrest onless ye'll agree t' git out o' the mountings t'-night."

Hippy shrugged his shoulders, and the Overlanders, with the exception of Grace, looked serious. Grace was trying hard not to laugh out loud.

"See here, Mister Man!" demanded Lieutenant Wingate gruffly. "My great grandfather was from Missouri. You have got to show me. How do I know you are a constable? Where is your authority?"

"This 'ere's mah authority," replied the mountaineer, patting his revolver holster.

Hippy stepped a little closer to the constable.

"And 'this 'ere's my authority' for saying that you are no more a constable than I am!" retorted the Overlander.

### *Whack!*

Hippy's fist landed on the point of the mountaineer's jaw, and the mountaineer went over backwards, landing heavily on the ground unconscious from the blow.

"Hippy! Oh, Hippy darlin'! What have you done?" wailed Nora.

"Hit him! Hit him again before he can get up!" cried Emma excitedly.

"Be quiet, you little savage," admonished Anne.

"You surely have done it this time, Hippy Wingate. Now we *are* in for trouble," rebuked Grace Harlowe.

"Brown Eyes, this fellow is a rank fraud. He isn't a constable, and I will wager that, were he to think there were such an animal within a mile of him, he would hit out for the bushes right smart."

"I agree with you. But, Hippy, you shouldn't have done that. The man was only bluffing. I saw that, or thought I did."

"So was I bluffing. The difference is that he and I do not bluff in the same way. Wait!" Hippy snatched the mountaineer's revolver from its holster, removed the cartridges and tossed them away, after which he returned the weapon to its holster. He then unbuckled the man's ammunition belt, shook all the cartridges out of that and rebuckled the belt about the fellow's waist.

"Laundry!" called Lieutenant Wingate.

"Yassuh! Yassuh!"

"Fetch me a pail of water. On the run!"

"I reckon this will wake him up," chuckled Hippy as he dashed the pailful of water that Washington brought, full into the face of the unconscious "constable."

It did. The man gasped and choked and struggled, and sat up, brushing the water out of his eyes with a sleeve. His blinking eyes slowly swept the camp, finally coming to rest on Hippy Wingate's face.

"Question him," suggested Grace.

"Who sent you here to try to bluff us?" asked Hippy sternly.

"Ah'll show ye." The mountain man's revolver was out of its holster in a flash as he leaped to his feet, and aimed it at Hippy. He pulled the trigger, but there was no report, only the click of the hammer as it struck the rim of an empty chamber of the revolver.

Five times did the fellow pull the trigger of his weapon, but with no better result, Hippy standing at ease before him, a smile on his face.

"I have a perfect right to shoot you for that, Mister 'Constable.' I may yet decide to do so. Who sent you here to play tricks on us?"

Uttering an exclamation of disgust, the mountain man thrust his revolver into its holster, one hand having crept about his ammunition belt and found it empty. He appeared to be dazed, but whether from the rap Hippy had given him, or because of the mysterious disappearance of his cartridges, they were not certain.

"Are you going to answer my question?"

The fellow shook his head.

"Do you know Jed Thompson?"

The mountaineer regarded his questioner sullenly, scowlingly, and without much change of expression. The scowl had been there ever since he woke up from the blow on his chin.

"Perhaps you know Bat Spurgeon?" This was one of the two names that Hippy had heard mentioned when he was the captive of the mountaineers. The other name was Jed Thompson, the man, undoubtedly, on whose farm the Overland Riders were then encamped.

A sudden change of expression flashed into the eyes of the "constable."

"So? You do know him, eh?" chuckled Lieutenant Wingate. Hippy drew his own weapon from its holster, fingering it absently while frowningly regarding the man before him.

"Why are you ruffians so eager to have us get out of the mountains? What have we done to you that you should be so dead set on getting rid of us?"

As before, there was no answer.

"I see it is useless to question you. Of course I could *make* you talk, and I would were there no ladies present to criticize my methods. However, I am going to let you go. You go back to the fellow who sent you here. Tell him for me that, if he bothers us further, we will take matters into our own hands. As for you, you poor fish, if ever I see you hanging about this or any other camp I am in, I'll shoot you on sight."

"Do it now while you have the chance," urged Emma.

Grace rebuked her with a stern look.

"I will give you ten seconds, after you have faced about, to get out of sight in the bushes," resumed Hippy. "Turn around! Go!"

**Bang!**

Hippy fired a shot over the head of the mountaineer who had fairly leaped for the bushes and disappeared in them.

"Quick! Follow him, darlin'. He may have other cartridges in his pockets," urged Nora.

"Anyway, the joke is on us. We fed the man and put evidence against us right in his stomach," wailed Emma Dean.

# CHAPTER XVII
# THE DANCE AT COON HOLLOW

Lieutenant Wingate, comprehending instantly, sprang into the bushes after the man he had driven out of camp.

"Didn't I tell you to get out of here?" demanded Hippy, pointing his revolver at the mountaineer, who had halted and was feverishly going through his pockets in search of ammunition.

The man stood not upon the order of his going, and, to speed him up, Lieutenant Wingate sent two shots over his head, following these up by chasing the fellow clear out into the open field where the Thompson cabin stood. The mountaineer made a quick run across the field, zigzagging, expecting, undoubtedly, to hear a bullet whistle past his head.

"Whew!" exclaimed the lieutenant, brushing the perspiration from his forehead as he stepped into the camp. "I am afraid I am not getting proper nourishment. My wind is not as good as it used to be. Nora darling, you will have to feed your husband better if you expect him to live this strenuous life."

"Did you hit him?" questioned Emma eagerly.

"No."

"Fiddlesticks! If I could not shoot straighter than that I think I should practice until I learned how to shoot."

"No you wouldn't. You would just sit down and 'con-centrate,'" retorted Hippy Wingate. "What do you make of all this, Brown Eyes?"

"More than I can very well express."

"I wish you might have been willing for me to use on him some of the methods employed by the intelligence department of the army to make Boche prisoners talk. He would talk, all right," said Hippy.

"This is not war," reminded Grace.

"No, but it is going to be," answered Hippy briefly. "Well, what do you dope out?"

"I think that the man who was just here is a Thompson man. Did you notice his expression when you mentioned Bat Spurgeon? If ever there was murder in a man's eyes, there was in his."

Hippy nodded.

"From what you overheard the night you were a captive of the mountaineers, you understood that the Spurgeons were going to start trouble with Jed Thompson, did you not?"

"Yes. Of course that may have been mere bluff talk," said Hippy.

"I don't think so. They are a bad lot, all of them. I am glad we have decided to leave this place, for, having assaulted our visitor, we may look for reprisals from Thompson."

"What's the difference? There is a price on my head, so I might as well be a lion as a lamb. Is there any bear meat left?"

"None cooked," replied Nora. "The 'constable' ate it all."

"I hope it gives him indigestion for life," growled Hippy. "I will watch the camp to-night, and, if you hear a rifle fired, don't get excited. It will be the man-with-a-price-on-his-head taking a pot shot at some fellow who is trying to earn the reward."

The Overland Riders did not sleep very well that night, for each of them looked for action from the mountain men. Nothing, however, occurred to disturb the camp.

Next morning Lieutenant Wingate went to the Thompson cabin to get milk, hoping to see Jed Thompson and have a talk with him, but Julie said "Paw" was not at home and might not be for "a right smart time."

While at the cabin, Lieutenant Wingate inquired how to reach the school-house in Coon Hollow where the dance was to be held that night. Julie told him in such great detail that Hippy was positive he never should find his way there, but he promised to do his best to get there.

"Ah'd go 'long and show you-all the way if Ah didn't have t' meet mah fellow. Bet you-all'll like him. Name's Lum Bangs an' he kin wallop any fellow in the mountains."

"Do you think he could whip me?" teased Hippy smilingly.

"He shore could. Jist let him lam you-all t'-night and see whether he kin er not."

"Thank you. I prefer to do the 'lamming' myself. When 'Paw' comes home please tell him I wish he would call on us to-day, for we are planning on moving our camp to-morrow. Tell him I wish to have a friendly talk with him."

Julie shook her head vigorously.

"Paw ain't strong on that kind o' talk. He'd rather fit with a man than gab with him."

Lieutenant Wingate asked Julie if she would dance with him, saying that Nora would be glad to have Julie do that.

"Ah will not," she retorted with a fine show of indignation.

"Why not?" teased Hippy.

"'Cause my feller would lam you-all's haid off an' then give me er punch in the jaw."

"Gracious! Lum is a gentle animal, isn't he?" grinned Hippy.

Julie blinked, but made no reply. Hippy said good-bye and went away laughing.

Late that afternoon Grace sent Washington out to learn the way to the schoolhouse, for, otherwise, she knew they would have difficulty in finding their way, for the nights up in the mountains just now were very dark.

Upon his return, the colored boy was unable to give them clear directions as to how to reach the schoolhouse, though his conversation on the subject was voluble, if not specific.

"That will do," rebuked Grace. "Pack all the supplies, except what will be needed for supper." She then consulted with Lieutenant Wingate as to where to stow their possessions so that they might not be disturbed by man or beast during the absence of the party at the mountain dance. Hippy went out and scouted about for a suitable place for the purpose. He found it in a hollow in the rocks which he said they could protect by placing stones in front of the opening.

Much of the equipment was stowed there before dark. After supper the rest of it was placed in the opening in the rocks.

"Do we take the rifles with us?" questioned Lieutenant Wingate.

"No, indeed," answered Grace with promptness. "It would not look well."

"Nor does it feel well to be held up or shot at without having the means to defend one's self," answered Hippy. "I shall take my revolver."

"Yes," agreed Grace. "Wear it under your blouse. I will do the same."

They decided to hide the rifles and ammunition in the bushes and trust to luck that no one stumbled on them. When they had finished with their preparations, nothing was left in the camp but the tents and a few blankets, mess kits and provisions being in the cache in the rocks.

One mule was to be ridden by Washington, the other to be left to its fate, hidden in a dense growth of laurel.

"I suppose he will awaken the whole country with his brays," growled Hippy.

"There are mules and mules," observed Emma Dean.

Hippy gave her a quick, keen glance, but her face was guileless.

At eight o'clock the Overland Riders set out on their ponies, Washington Washington in the lead on his pack mule, industriously mouthing his harmonica, the girls laughing and chatting, Hippy silent, lost in contemplation of his own problems.

"Which way to the Coon Hollow schoolhouse?" called Grace as they passed a slowly walking couple a short distance beyond the Thompson home.

"Yer headin' fer it," answered the man.

"If Laundry gives the mule a free rein, we probably shall reach our destination sooner than if the boy tries to guide the animal," suggested Elfreda Briggs.

As they neared the schoolhouse they heard the music of the "band," as Julie had been pleased to call it. Hearing, Washington Washington played his own musical instrument with renewed vigor.

Many others, bound toward the schoolhouse, laughed and made remarks, or greeted the Overlanders pleasantly as they passed.

The ponies and the mule were tethered to trees hard by the schoolhouse, after which the party filed into the building, with Washington trailing along after them, rolling his eyes and wagging his head in rhythm with the music of violin and banjo.

The music proved too much for Washington to endure in silence, and the Overland Riders were amazed when he clapped the harmonica to his lips and began to play with the two musicians.

Grace started for the boy, but another got to him ahead of her. A young mountaineer picked up the colored boy and tossed him out through a window. It was not so roughly done that the Overlanders could make a protest, and the young fellow who had performed the feat turned from the window laughing over the neat way he had checked Washington's musical interference.

The dance already was under full headway. The floor swayed and groaned, and the building fairly rocked under the rhythmic assault of more than twenty pairs of stamping, shuffling feet. A smoking oil lamp supplied a dull, smoky haze so that it was difficult for friends to recognize each other from opposite ends of the room. All eyes, including those of the dancers, had been turned to the newcomers as the Overlanders filed in and took seats on benches at one side of the room.

It was but a few moments later when Hippy and Nora swung out on the floor and Hippy was soon raising the dust with the best of them.

He then danced with each of the girls of his party in turn. Grace, watching the unusual scene with keen interest, observed that there was little or no change of partners. Each young mountaineer danced with the same girl most of the time, and she concluded that this was the custom up there in the mountains.

At the end of the first dance after their arrival, Grace called Emma over to her.

"I brought two boxes of candy with me, Emma," she whispered. "There is one box left at the camp and I wish to give that to the Thompson children. Do you wish to pass these two boxes around to the mountain girls?"

Emma was delighted. It gave her an opportunity to place herself in a more prominent position than she had occupied on a bench at the side of the school-room.

At first the mountain girls were shy, but they soon overcame their diffidence and helped themselves liberally--by the handful--to sweets such as few of them ever had tasted.

"This is Mrs. Gray's treat," explained Emma to each girl.

"Don't Ah git any?" teased the young mountaineer who had assisted Washington through the window.

"Yes. You get left," came back Emma spiritedly.

"Ah never gits left," he retorted, springing up and grabbing the little Overland girl.

In a few seconds they were swinging around the room in a waltz, Emma's face flushed and triumphant, the face of the partner of the man she was dancing with growing blacker with the moments. The mountaineer would not release Emma until she had danced two dances with him, and by that time the girl he had brought to the party refused even to look at him.

Emma made her unsought partner introduce her to other boys, and with smiles and teasing she won many partners, until the room was bordered with a ring of blazing and snapping eyes, all resentful at her success in winning their escorts.

Grace tried to catch her eye to warn her, but Emma studiously refrained from permitting that very thing. Soon the mountain girls allowed themselves to be led to the dancing floor by others than their own escorts.

The atmosphere was becoming highly charged. Even Hippy had swung a mountain miss out to the floor and was dancing with her, but the Overland girls, with the exception of Emma, had smilingly declined when invited by mountain boys to dance.

Men, under the scornful smiles on the faces of their regular partners, were growing sullen. The laughter was dying from the faces of the dancers, and it was quite evident that trouble was brewing.

"Call Hippy to you and tell him to sit down by you, Nora," whispered Grace Harlowe. "I will catch Emma at the end of this dance, if I can. That child is going to start a riot if she is allowed to go on much longer."

Hippy got his summons a few moments thereafter. He obeyed it as gracefully as he could, but rather against his inclinations, for he was having a jolly time of it, forgetting for the moment that he was "a marked man."

Grace explained the situation briefly to Hippy, and told him that between himself and Emma they had created a situation that bade fair to end in trouble.

"What's the odds? I am a marked man anyway," answered Hippy, shrugging his shoulders.

"You will be marked in reality if those husky young mountaineers get after you. Please keep your seat and fade out of the picture," urged Grace. "You see--"

A voice to one side of her arrested Grace Harlowe's attention. She recognized it as the voice of Julie Thompson, whom she had not seen at the dance up to that time, though she had been looking for her.

"Oh, Mr. Hipp," Julie was saying. "Ah wants t' give you-all a knockdown to mah feller. Oh, here's Miss Gray, too. Folks, this is my feller, Lum Bangs."

"Sounds like a pain in the back," muttered Hippy.

"Lum, shake paws with Mister Hipp an' Miss Gray. They're the folks that air campin' down by Paw's cornfield."

"Glad to meet you, Lum, for we all think Julie is a mighty fine--" Hippy's voice trailed off into an indistinct murmur as he gazed up into the face of Julie's stalwart escort. He heard Grace give utterance to a scarcely audible laugh, but at that moment Hippy Wingate did not feel like laughter, for in Lum Bangs he recognized the "constable" whom he had knocked down and driven from the Overland camp by the cornfield.

# CHAPTER XVIII
# AN INTERRUPTED PARTY

Oh! It's you, is it?" muttered Lieutenant Wingate, rising slowly, his eyes fixed on the face of the man before him.

"Ah reckons as it's me," agreed Lum, permitting a hand to slip carelessly inside his coat across the chest, where Lieutenant Wingate had reason to believe that a revolver hung suspended from a shoulder holster. This being the case, he considered it inadvisable to reach for his own weapon.

As yet the drama being played by the two men had not attracted the attention of those in the schoolroom, with the exception of the Overland girls who had recognized Lum instantly, and Julie Thompson, who was gazing open-mouthed from one to the other of them.

"Ah told ye t' git out, didn't Ah?" demanded the mountaineer in a strained voice.

"And I put you out," retorted Hippy. "This is no place for a fight. If you wish to see me, come around to our camp in the morning."

"Be careful, Hippy," warned Anne in a low tone.

"Ah'm goin' t' say it agin, once more. You git out o' this right smart or Ah'll put er hole through yer miserable carcass!"

Hippy suddenly found himself facing a revolver in the hands of Lum Bangs.

The dancers stopped dancing, a couple at a time, and quickly got out of range of Lum Bangs' weapon; the music died away, and a heavy silence, tense with possibilities, settled over the hot, smoky room.

"Are ye goin'?"

"On one condition--that you put down your gun and come outside with me. We'll have it out man to man. These gentlemen will give us fair play, and the fellow who is whipped takes his medicine and goes. Are you man enough to come out and stand up to me?" Hippy thrust out his chin, and there was a set expression on his face, such as Grace Harlowe recalled having seen there immediately after he had shot down three German airplanes on the French fighting front.

"No, no!" begged Nora, not much above a whisper.

"Oh, stop him!" begged Emma of the young mountaineer with whom she had been dancing. "He's going to shoot. I know he is. Make them fight it out with their fists. Hippy whipped Lum once, and he can do it again. I'll be Lum's second and you can be the second for Lieutenant Wingate."

"What's er second, Miss?"

"A--a second is one who fans his fighter with a towel, and wipes up the blood. Oh, do stop him!"

"Ah reckon Ah will," drawled the mountaineer.

"Are ye goin'?" demanded Lum Bangs.

"No!"

"Drop that gun or I'll drill ye, Lum Bangs!" commanded the cool voice of Emma Dean's dancing partner, his revolver now levelled at Lum.

The warning came too late.

Lum Bangs, in a sudden impulse of rage, pulled the trigger and fired point blank at Lieutenant Wingate, but the young mountaineer's warning to him, at the critical moment, had drawn Lum's thoughts from his aim, and his bullet missed its mark. Hippy heard it whistle past him close to his head.

***Bang!***

Barely a second had elapsed between Lum Bangs' shot and a second report.

Lum uttered a howl, and his weapon dropped from his relaxed fingers, just as Hippy sprang upon him and dealt the mountaineer a blow that felled him.

"Don't! Don't, Hippy! The man has been shot," begged Anne.

"Jump on him! Stomp on him, why don't ye?" screamed a mountain girl.

The room was in instant uproar, and weapons were drawn and levelled menacingly at the young mountaineer who had ordered Lum to "drop" his gun.

"Stop!" cried Emma Dean excitedly. "This man didn't fire that second shot. He has done nothing, so put away your cannon."

"That's right, folks. Ah didn't shoot, but Ah was goin' t'. Some other duffer fired the shot that hit Lum. You-all kin look at mah gun." He held it out with the muzzle toward him.

The men crowded about him, examining the cylinder to see if a cartridge had been fired from it, and taking a sniff at the muzzle.

"That's right. It ain't been fired," agreed a mountaineer, a puzzled expression appearing on his face. "Did Lum get his'n?"

"No. The bullet went through his wrist," answered Lieutenant Wingate, who, having turned up the sleeve of Bangs' coat, was peering at the wounded wrist. "Men, I'm sorry I struck him, but you see I didn't know some one was going to shoot him. I had to punch him to save my own life, expecting that he would shoot again. As it was I nearly ran into that second shot. Fetch me something--some water."

A glass of lemonade was brought, and Nora Wingate threw it into the face of the unconscious mountaineer. In the meantime, Elfreda was giving first aid to the injured wrist. Lum began to stir about this time, and, at Elfreda's suggestion, he was carried to a window where he might get more free air.

The mountaineers were puzzled. They had, by then, examined every revolver in the room, including those carried by the Overland Riders, but not one had been fired.

"Ah wants ter know who fired that shot," demanded one of them. "Somebody did, an' we're goin' to find the critter that did it. I ain't sayin' that this feller with the uniform on didn't do all right in hittin' Lum, but what we wants t' find out is who winged him in the wrist."

"I think, gentlemen, that the second shot was fired through the window. I am quite certain that it was. I sat near the window and the report of the weapon seemed to be behind me," Anne Nesbit informed them.

There was a concerted rush for the outer air, leaving the Overlanders to attend to Lum Bangs, who was now almost wholly restored to consciousness. Julie Thompson was standing back a little from the group about him, gazing at Lum, a heavy frown on her forehead. Grace nodded and smiled to the girl.

"Don't worry, Julie. He will be all right in a few moments," soothed the Overland girl.

"I ain't worryin' fer the likes o' him," she replied, elevating her chin and turning her back on her escort.

The Overland girls looked at each other inquiringly.

"Ah hearn somethin' 'bout ye to-night, Lum Bangs, that ye don't know as Ah does know," she said, whirling suddenly on him.

"You-all ain't goin' back on me, are yuh, Julie?" begged Lum.

"Naw. Ah ain't goin' back on ye, cause Ah already has. Ah don't want nothin' more t' do with ye. Understand?"

The mountaineer's face reddened.

"Who shot me?" he demanded, sitting up suddenly and feeling for his weapon.

"You needn't look at me that way," objected Hippy. "I didn't shoot you. I punched you, that's all. Some one on the outside of the building fired the shot that hit you. I--"

A commotion at the door interrupted Hippy. The mountaineers came crowding in dragging Washington Washington with them. Washington's eyes were rolling, and he was trembling from fright.

"Is this heah your niggah?" demanded one, glaring at Hippy.

"No, he isn't my 'niggah,' but he belongs to our outfit. Why?" replied Lieutenant Wingate.

"'Cause we found him hidin' in the bushes, an' reckoned as mebby he is the feller that shot Lum."

"What, Wash?" laughed Emma Dean. "Why, Wash couldn't hit the side of a barn with a shotgun. Besides, he has no revolver, and it was a revolver that fired the shot you refer to."

"Let me talk to him," urged Grace. "Washington, were you outside near the building when the shots were fired?" she asked in a soothing tone.

"Yessah--yes'm."

"Did you see any one near the window?"

"Yessah--yes'm. Ah--Ah sawed er man hidin' in de bush dere."

"Did you see him shoot?" asked Elfreda.

"Ah did not, but Ah heard him shoot, den w'en Ah looked, Ah didn't sawed him no moah."

"Who was it?" demanded a mountaineer.

"Ah doan know. Ah didn't sawed him close 'nuf, an' den Ah didn't sawed him at all."

"He oughter be strung up anyway," suggested a voice.

"Don't get excited! Don't get excited," urged Lieutenant Wingate, when it became plain that the mountaineers were determined to make further trouble.

"Gentlemen, Lieutenant Wingate has given you good advice. That colored boy is not to be blamed for what has occurred here," declared Miss Briggs, getting to her feet. "It is not necessary for you to take my word for that, nor the boy's. You can prove it for yourselves."

"How?" demanded several voices.

"Go outside and examine the bushes that grow by the window through which the shot was fired, and look at the ground carefully for foot-tracks. I am amazed that you didn't think of it yourselves. You see when one is angry he does not reason and--"

The men did not give her opportunity to finish. They again bolted from the schoolroom. Their voices and their exclamations were heard under the window a moment later.

"That was fine, J. Elfreda," glowed Grace.

"If they fail to find tracks there I am sorry for Wash, that's all," replied Miss Briggs with a shrug.

"Yer right!" cried a mountaineer, entering the room at that juncture. "We seen where the critter was standin' when he shot Lum. We seen the mark o' his boots, and the bunch is startin' to follow his trail. Reckon you gals might as well go home, fer they'll be a different kind o' a party if they kotch him. Won't be no more dancin' t'-night."

"Ladies, I am sorry if we were the cause of trouble here," began Grace.

"You-all ain't," protested Julie.

"Thank you." Grace favored her with a radiant smile. "What I was about to say, is that we expect to break camp and go on to-morrow morning. If we do not, we should like to have you young ladies come and call on us. It is always open house in the Overland camp. Julie, I hope we shall see you in the morning."

"Ah don't reckon as you-all will be goin' away in the mornin'. Ah s'ppose Ah ought t' tell you-all what Ah knows, but Ah reckons you-all'll find out for yourselves soon 'nuf."

Julie's words did not impress the Overlanders at the moment, but while on their way to camp they pondered over them, discussed them and wondered what she may have meant.

The answer to the question in their minds Grace and her friends found awaiting them when they reached the camp.

# CHAPTER XIX
# A CALL FOR HELP

Hippy, did you know that I saved your life to-night?" asked Emma Dean as the party neared their camp.

"You--you saved my life?" questioned Lieutenant Wingate in amazement.

"Uh-huh."

Hippy laughed uproariously.

"You poor child, you got us all in Dutch, that's what you really did."

"With your assistance, Hippy," interjected Anne. "How did you save his life, please, Emma?"

"I con-centrated. When Lum pointed the revolver at Hippy, I put my mind on making him miss his aim. He did, didn't he?"

"Yes," agreed the girls, Hippy saying nothing at all.

"Then, I con-centrated on him that he might not shoot again. He didn't, did he?"

"Of course, you are right in what you say," agreed Nora. "He did miss and he did not shoot again, but I think you are drawing the long bow, darlin', in taking all the credit to yourself. What do you say, Hippy?" she asked solemnly.

"Nothing! Nothing at all. After I have had an opportunity to consult a dictionary perhaps I may make a few appropriate remarks."

The party, with the exception of Emma, after a hearty laugh, fell to discussing the incidents of the evening, particularly the mysterious shot that, perhaps, had saved Lieutenant Wingate's life. They were still discussing that mysterious occurrence when they rode up to their camp.

Washington Washington, who had been silent all the way home, perhaps thinking over the narrow escape that he had had from rough handling, suddenly set up a wail and began to chatter so fast that they were unable to make a single thing of what he was saying.

"Stop that!" commanded Hippy. "Have you gone crazy?"

"Something is wrong here, darlin'. Don't scold the boy," begged Nora Wingate.

"The tents are down. Washington, build a fire. Be quick about it," directed Grace, leaping from her pony.

Anne, who had reached what had been her own tent, uttered an exclamation of dismay.

"Girls, this tent has been slit into ribbons!" she cried.

"So has mine," cried Elfreda. "What has happened here?"

"That is what I am wondering," replied Grace. "Washington, please hurry with that fire."

Hippy ran over and assisted the colored boy, who was fumbling about and not accomplishing anything. In a few moments Hippy had a fire snapping. By its light they looked about in amazement. The camp was a wreck. Every tent in their outfit had been slit to pieces, tent poles had been broken up, and such other equipment as they had left out, including three blankets, which had been overlooked when they hid their belongings, had been practically destroyed.

A sudden thought occurring to her, Anne ran on fleet feet to the place where their provisions and equipment had been secreted. She found the stones torn away from the opening and their supplies scattered about. The ground about the opening to the hiding place was littered with them.

Her next move was to look for their rifles and ammunition. A moment later she ran breathlessly into camp.

"The equipment has been scattered, but the rifles and ammunition are as we left them," panted Anne. "This is a fright."

"There! Why didn't you 'con-centrate,' Emma Dean?" demanded Hippy. "Old Con-centration is never on the job when he is really needed."

"How could I when I didn't know anything about this?" returned Emma, with a sweeping gesture that took in the entire camp. "What are we going to do now? Where are we to sleep, I ask you?"

"Sleep standing up just as the ponies do, my darlin'," suggested Nora. "Who do you suppose could have done such a thing? Why--"

Washington, who had gone out to tether the horses, set up a howl that called the Overlanders to him on a run.

"Dey done got de mule! Dey done got de mule!" he wailed. "What Ah gwine do now? Ah doan like dis nohow. Ah sure gwine took er frenzy spell if dis doan stop right smart."

"The mule?" gasped Anne. "Why--wha--"

The pack mule that had been left at the camp, they saw laying stretched out on the ground, its halter still tied to a sapling. Hippy was now standing over it, peering down at the animal. Stooping over, he examined it briefly.

"Somebody has done it this time. The mule is dead, folks," he announced, standing up. "Shot through the head. It seems our *friends* have not yet deserted us."

"This is an outrage!" muttered Elfreda.

Grace turned on her lamp and went over the ground about the mule, examining the dirt for footprints as carefully as possible. Next she visited the hiding place of their provisions and equipment, there to make the same careful, painstaking search of the ground.

"Hob-nail boots. I find the imprint of the same boots in both places. One man apparently did all of this," was her conclusion.

"Such as all these mountaineers wear," added Anne.

"Perhaps, but I do not believe it. These boots had a horseshoe of hob-nails on each heel. Look at the footprints in the morning and see for yourself."

"Wait!" exclaimed Miss Briggs. "I have a thought."

"Hold it," called Hippy. "We need real thought this very minute."

"Have you forgotten what Julie said to us?" asked Elfreda. "I believe this is what she meant by her remark that we would find out for ourselves soon enough."

"She knew, then!" exclaimed Nora.

"I believe she did, though how, I am at a loss to understand," answered Elfreda.

"Girls, girls! Don't waste time talking," urged Grace. "We have work to do, unless you folks prefer to sleep in the open to-night. I believe we can mend enough of this canvas to use as a big blanket. We can then sleep together and keep each other warm underneath it, I think. Washington, please go out and gather up all of the stuff that you can find. Some of our provisions have been destroyed, but there may be enough for a few meals. Fetch everything here so we can look it over by the campfire."

All hands set to work to make the best of their disaster, and as they worked they discussed the problem uppermost in the mind of each. They were busily engaged when a shout brought instant silence to the group.

"Miss Gray! Miss Gray!" some one called from the darkness.

"Yes," answered Grace.

A woman came floundering along the trail at the edge of the cornfield.

"It's Miss Thompson. Ah wants Miss Gray."

"She seems excited," observed Emma.

"What is it, Mrs. Thompson?" called Grace, stepping out to meet the mountaineer's wife.

"The chilern has took a frenzy, an' Ah don't know what t' do," cried the woman, wringing her hands.

Slipping an arm through hers, Grace led the woman up to the campfire.

"Compose yourself. Now what is the trouble? Are the children sick?" she asked.

"Yes'm. An' Jed's gone away an' Ah don't know what t' do. Ah thought as mebby ye'd come up to the house an' see."

"I surely will. Miss Briggs, who was a nurse in the war, will be of more assistance to you than I could be, so I will take her with me."

Jed Thompson's wife heaved a deep sigh. A load already had been lifted from her mind.

"Ah didn't think ye'd come, but Julie said as you'd come right smart."

"Julie was right," smiled Grace, "even though we are in rather bad shape here. Some one nearly destroyed our camp while we were at the dance. I will be back before long," she added, speaking to her companions. "Come, Elfreda."

On the way to the Thompson cabin the two girls questioned Mrs. Thompson as to what ailed Lizzie and Sue, those being the names of the two sick children. They were able to make but little out of her description of the children's condition.

The sick ones were babbling when Grace and Miss Briggs entered the room.

Elfreda sniffed the air.

"I smell fever. Open the windows, Mrs. Thompson. You must have air in this room."

Julie, her face wearing a frightened look, sat regarding the children, both of whom were delirious. A look of relief flashed into her eyes as Grace and Miss Briggs entered and Elfreda stepped directly to the bed on which both children lay. She felt the pulse of each, looked into their mouths, and listened to their breathing.

"High fever?" murmured Grace questioningly.

"Yes. Very high. I wish I had a clinical thermometer. Make her throw those windows open as far as they will go, and, if that doesn't give enough air, open the door."

The entire family lived, ate and slept in the one room of the cabin, and the air, normally bad enough, was infinitely worse now.

"How long have they been this way, Mrs. Thompson?" questioned Elfreda.

"They was took that-away t'-night. They ain't been right smart fer some little time."

Miss Briggs and Grace consulted aside. At the conclusion of their consultation, carried on in low tones, Elfreda turned to the mountain woman.

"These children must have a doctor without delay, Mrs. Thompson. Where is the nearest doctor to be found?"

The woman said the nearest one was at Holcomb Court House.

"We passed through there on our way here, did we not?" asked Elfreda.

"Yes," replied Grace. "It must be twenty miles or so from here. Have you any one that you can send there for the doctor?"

Mrs. Thompson shook her head.

"Mah man's gone awa' an' won't be back till t'-morrow. Ain't no one else that Ah knows 'bout."

"Do you think it would be safe to wait until morning, Elfreda?" asked Grace.

"No. The little one's heart is not acting right. We must have treatment for her as soon as possible."

"Very well. I will hurry back to camp. Hippy must go after the doctor, though I really hate to ask him. What do you think is the matter with them?" nodding toward the bed.

"Frankly, I don't know. I do know that they are very sick children."

"Poor Hippy," murmured Grace, a faint smile on her face, as she hurried from the mountain cabin and started at a run towards the Overland Riders' camp.

# CHAPTER XX
# HIPPY AS A ROUGHRIDER

Reaching her camp, Grace quickly acquainted the girls with conditions at the Thompson cabin. She then turned to Hippy and told him that he must ride to Holcomb Court House and fetch a doctor.

"All right. I'll get an early start in the morning and--"

"No! To-night! Now, Hippy. To-morrow may be too late," urged Grace.

"Of course, if it is so bad as that. Why don't you have Emma Dean 'con-cen-trate'?"

"This is not a matter to make light of, Hippy Wingate," rebuked Nora. "Of course you will go."

"Laundry, get my pony, and be lively about it," ordered Lieutenant Wingate.

While this was being done, and Hippy was looking to his rifle and revolver, Grace was explaining to him how to reach Holcomb over the broad wagon trail that they had followed during the last day of their journey. Nora, in the meantime, was packing her husband's kit with sufficient food, that had been picked up from the scattered remnants, to see him through the trip. Twenty minutes later they had started Hippy on his way.

"If I don't come back, remember that I had a price on my head," he called back to his companions.

"Pack up!" directed Grace. "We must move up near the Thompson cabin. It won't do for you girls to remain here alone."

"Where shall we camp?" asked Anne, a worried look on her face. "We have no tents fit for use."

"I don't know just yet, but they have a barn. Perhaps you might sleep there. I must stay with Elfreda, at least until the doctor comes."

All the girls began to prepare for moving, and finally their possessions were strapped in packs, some of which they placed on the backs of ponies, for they were one mule short, and moved up to Thompson's.

Bidding her companions wait outside, Grace went in and consulted with the mountaineer's wife.

"Yes, you folks will have to sleep in the barn," Grace informed them.

"I never thought I should have to sleep with the pigs and the cows," declared Nora. "Bad luck to the man that spoiled our fun."

There was an old haymow overhead in the barn, and there the girls decided to make their bed for the night.

"If there are mice up here I shall die of fright, I know," groaned Emma.

"'Con-centrate' on the mice," advised Anne teasingly. "Once they bump against that 'imponderable quantity,' the mice will trouble you no more."

"Why can't we go into the cabin and lie down on the floor? It can't be worse than the barn," urged Nora.

Grace firmly refused to permit it. Not knowing what the two children were suffering from, she knew that it would be inadvisable for her companions even to enter the cabin.

The girls found their way to the hayloft, after many bumps and falls accompanied by smothered cries and loud protests from Emma, and after he had tethered the horses and the mule just outside the barn, Washington Washington was put to bed on the barn floor. Grace then returned to the cabin.

The children were still delirious and Elfreda said that their temperature seemed to be rising. She decided to give them a sponge bath. This occupied some time, but it had the effect of reducing their temperatures somewhat.

Julie watched every movement of the Overland nurses, following them with eyes in which wonder was not unmixed with admiration, but Mrs. Thompson seemed helpless to do or think, and sat regarding them with expressionless eyes, now and then heaving a troubled sigh.

Along towards morning the children ceased their babbling and sank into an uneasy sleep. The mother, soon after, dozed off in her chair.

"Julie, get some water and soap and help us clean this place. It's a fright," declared Miss Briggs.

This Julie did, so far as getting the water was concerned, but she took so little interest in scrubbing the floor that Grace and Elfreda were obliged to take that task into their own hands. They were down on their knees scrubbing away, when Mrs. Thompson awakened.

"What you-all doin'?" she demanded blinkingly.

"Cleaning house," replied Elfreda briefly.

"'Tain't no use. It'll git dirty ag'in. Ah reckon Jed won't like it, neither."

"We don't care whether Jed likes it or not," retorted Grace. "Leave him to us, Mrs. Thompson."

Early in the morning Grace and Elfreda went out to the barn to see how it had fared with their friends. They were a "frowzy lot," as Miss Briggs characterized their appearance. Their heads were full of hay, their eyes were red, and their faces showed much loss of sleep.

"You folks go down to the brook and wash, and by the time you return we shall have breakfast cooked for you," offered Elfreda.

The breakfast they cooked on Mrs. Thompson's stove, but in the Overlanders' utensils. Nor would they permit any of the girls to come into the house for the food. Handing the breakfast out to the eagerly waiting hands of their companions, Grace and Miss Briggs soon followed and joined the girls at breakfast in the open.

It was not a particularly enjoyable meal. Not once during the breakfast had one mentioned Hippy Wingate and his mission, and it was not until they had finished and sat back that Nora broached the subject.

"When should Hippy be back?" she asked.

"If he found the doctor at once he should have been here two or three hours ago," replied Grace.

"Don't get excited, Nora," begged Elfreda, as Nora's face paled ever so little. "A number of things may have occurred to detain him. Hippy is not one to be beaten when he starts out with a definite purpose in view."

"Especially when I am con-centrating on him," spoke up Emma.

This brought a laugh and put all the girls in instant good humor. They were interrupted by Julie who came out rubbing her eyes, after a few hours' sleep on a blanket on the floor of the cabin.

"Maw wants to know what she'll give Sue and Liz fer breakfast?" she asked.

"Breakfast?" exclaimed Elfreda. "Not a mouthful until the doctor gets here and advises what is to be done. They may have all the water they wish, but nothing of solid food. You won't forget, will you?"

Julie shook her head.

"This is the first opportunity I have had to speak with you quietly since last night, Julie," said Grace. "You made a remark as we were about to leave the dance, indicating that you knew something had occurred at our camp. Julie, you knew what had been done there, didn't you?"

The mountain girl nodded.

"How did you know?"

"Er feller an' girl comin' t' the dance seen it," she answered with some hesitation.

"And you know who did it?"

"Uh-huh," nodded the girl.

"Who was it?"

"Ah shan't tell you-all!" exclaimed Julie, a challenge snapping in her black eyes.

"That is all right, my dear, if you do not wish to speak. How is your friend, Lum Bangs, to-day?"

"He ain't no friend of mine. Ah don't know nothin' 'bout how he is, an' Ah don't care." Julie blazed as she said it.

The Overland girls smiled. Grace's question, they thought, had been answered.

"Thar comes somebody," cried Julie, distracting the attention of all from the subject.

A man on horseback was seen pounding up the trail at a fast pace.

"It's the doc!" announced the mountain girl.

"Hippy! Where's Hippy?" gasped Nora.

"Keep steady," urged Grace, as they got up and walked out to meet the doctor in front of the cabin.

"Are you the doctor?" asked Elfreda as he rode up and swung a hand to them.

"Yes."

"Where did you leave Lieutenant Wingate?" asked Grace.

"About ten miles down the trail. I got here as quickly as possible. To be brief, we were attacked from ambush. The lieutenant's horse was shot from under him. We both began shooting, but he yelled to me, 'Go on, Doc. They need you at Thompson's. I'll get out of it somehow.'

"Well, I saw that he was right, so I rode for keeps till I got out of range of the bullets. Lively neighborhood up here, eh? I'll see the patients, if you please."

Elfreda conducted the doctor into the cabin, Grace remaining to comfort Nora and to consider what was best to be done in the circumstances. Nora was urging her to start out in search of Hippy, but Grace pointed out that they were as likely to miss as to find him, and that the best course appeared to be to wait until later in the day, then, should Lieutenant Wingate not return, a searching party must be organized to go out for him. Grace then entered the cottage and the girls led Nora out to the shady side of the barn where they consoled her as best they could.

"I will sit right down here and con-centrate," promised Emma. "You will see that it will fetch him back. If it doesn't never, never again will I con-centrate on Hippy. The trouble is that he resists the instant he feels the magnetic current, which makes con-centrating very difficult and takes so much of the imponderable quality out of one--"

"Emma! Emma!" cried Anne. "For mercy sake come up and get a breath of air. You will drown if you stay down another second."

Nora laughed heartily.

In the meantime Grace and Elfreda were leaning over the bed watching the doctor's diagnosis. Elfreda told him what had been done for the two children, naming the few home remedies that she had been able to find and administer to them.

"Good, Miss Lizzie might have been dead by this time if you had not done what you did. Susie is not in quite such bad shape."

"What is the matter with them?" questioned Grace.

"Scarlet fever--both of them," was the terse answer. "Have your party all been exposed?"

Elfreda informed him that, not knowing what the children's trouble was, they had thought best not to permit the Overland Riders to enter the cabin.

Grace questioned the doctor further on the attack that had been made on himself and Hippy, and asked him to indicate, as nearly as possible, the spot where the attack was made.

The doctor was giving them the details when the door of the cabin was roughly thrown open and a man stepped in.

"It's Paw! Hello, Paw. The Doc is here."

Jed Thompson carried a rifle under his arm, and his face was as black as a thunder cloud.

"Here's a squall," murmured Miss Briggs, just loud enough for Grace to hear.

"What you-all doin' here?" he demanded, eyeing the two Overland Riders sternly.

It was plain that Thompson's anger was rapidly getting the best of him.

"You-all! Git out o' mah house afore Ah throws ye out!" he roared.

"Be quiet, Paw," urged Julie weakly, Mrs. Thompson being too frightened to utter a word.

"When we have finished with our work, Mr. Thompson, we will leave. Not one second sooner," retorted Elfreda Briggs coolly, as she stepped forward and faced the irate mountaineer.

"Then Ah'll throw ye out! The pack of ye git out afore Ah fergits mahself and shoots ye out."

Jed started for Miss Briggs, his anger now beyond all control.

"Stop where you are, Jed Thompson!" commanded Elfreda Briggs.

The mountaineer halted abruptly. He was facing J. Elfreda's revolver, which was leveled at him, held in a steady hand.

"Let your rifle drop to the floor," she directed sweetly. "Drop it! My hand is a little nervous to-day and this revolver might go off."

The rifle clattered to the floor, but Elfreda Briggs still held her position, her eyes narrowly watching the angry mountaineer.

## CHAPTER XXI
## AN APOLOGY AND A THREAT

Here, here, here!" roared the doctor in a commanding voice. "What you-all trying to do here? Haven't you got trouble enough on hand without looking for more, Jed Thompson? Give me that gun."

The doctor recovered the fallen rifle, drew the cartridges from its magazine, dropped them in his pocket and stood the gun in a corner.

Elfreda lowered her weapon, but did not immediately return it to its holster under her blouse.

"Thank you," she said, smiling over at the doctor.

"Listen to me, Jed," ordered the doctor. "These young women came here to see what they could do for Sue and Liz. If they hadn't, Liz probably would be dead this minute. They saved her life, Jed Thompson. Now what have you got to say for yourself?"

"That right, Doc?"

"It's the almighty truth. That isn't all. Lieutenant Wingate, one of their party, rode all the way to Holcomb after me last night and nearly killed his horse. On the way back we were attacked from ambush and the lieutenant's horse was shot from under him. I tried to stick and help him fight the critters off, but he told me to 'get!' Said I was needed here. He's down there yet, maybe dead. Jed Thompson, you ought to get down on your knees and apologize to these women folk. I've half a notion to whale you if you don't."

Jed fumbled his hat.

"Who do you-all reckon did the attackin'?" he stammered.

"I don't know. You ought to know more about it than I do. You folks up here in the hills are altogether too sudden--too handy with your guns. One of these days you will meet some one who is more so."

"Ah reckons that young woman's kinder sudden, too," answered Jed, with a sheepish grin at Miss Briggs. "Do you-all say that some critter shot at that feller when he was fetchin' you-all here for Liz an' Sue?"

"Yes. They may have got him before this."

"Gi' me that rifle!" demanded the mountaineer sternly.

"Wait, Jed. What do you propose to do?" questioned the doctor.

"Ah'm goin' t' fetch the loot'nant, an' Ah'm goin' t' git the feller that shot you-all up if Ah kin kotch him."

"Take the rifle, Jed, and the best of luck," bowed the doctor, handing the weapon to the mountaineer, and reaching into his pocket for the cartridges he had taken from it. "We'll now see what we can do for the sick."

Jed was out of the house and across the field at top speed by the time Elfreda had reached the door, after stowing her revolver.

"He is right," nodded Grace, regarding Elfreda with sparkling eyes. "You *are* sudden. I did not think it was in you to be so quick."

"Huh! I was scared half to death. It is a wonder I didn't--"

"Of course we take that for granted," twinkled Grace.

The doctor announced that he would stay until the children got better, all day and night if necessary. There being nothing more for them to do for the time being, Grace and Elfreda joined their companions outside.

They had not been outside the cabin very long before Emma uttered a little cry of delight, and excitedly pointed down the trail that led past the cornfield.

"Look! Oh, look! There comes Hippy and Mr. Thompson. Didn't I tell you I would fetch Hippy back?" she cried.

"Why, Emma, how is that?" wondered Grace.

"I con-centrated on him, I did, and--"

"She did," glowed Nora, running forward to meet her husband.

"You should open an office when you get home," advised Miss Briggs. "Let me see, your business sign should read, 'Miss Dean, Imponderable Concentrator.'"

"Make all the fun you wish. I know now what I can do, and you know what I have done, only you folks are too stubborn to admit it." Emma elevated her chin and stamped around behind the barn out of sight.

After Hippy had embraced Nora and greeted the other girls he shook hands with the doctor, who had come to the cabin door to wave a hand at Hippy.

"They didn't get you after all, I see," chuckled the doctor.

Hippy grinned.

"Now you-all is back, Ah wants t' talk t' ye," said Jed.

"Just a minute, Jed. What's that, Doc?"

"I say, what happened after I left you?"

"We took a few pot shots at each other from the bushes. The bullets got rather thick, so I decided upon a retreat. Came near having another set-to with Jed. We both were stalking each other down the trail a piece, but Jed got the drop on me and, when he found out who I was, he told me that he had come after me and why."

The doctor chuckled and returned to his patients, whereupon Hippy nodded to the mountaineer, and the latter led the way to the rear of the barn where they found Emma sunning herself and "con-centrating" on something. Hippy waved her away and turned to Thompson.

"What's the big idea, Jed?" he asked jovially.

"That's what Ah wants t' know, Jim Townsend."

"Eh? Townsend! I don't get you."

"We uns up here ain't no fools even if we hain't got edication. We uns knowed you-all was comin'. If I'd seen ye before ye did this fer Liz an' Sue, I'd a plugged ye shore."

"Just a moment, please. Let me get this straight. Who is it you think I am?"

"Yer Jim Townsend. Ah knows you-all, cause you-all was pinted out t' me one time down t' Henderson, 'cept ye didn't have on them togs you-all is wearin' now."

"Who is Townsend?" questioned Hippy. "If he looks like me, he is a very fortunate man."

"You be he. What Ah wants t' know is what--jest what's yer game up here? As Ah've said, you-all, and the wimmen, has done me a favor an' no man kin say Jed Thompson ever fergits a favor. But it kain't last. You-all got ter git out. What Ah ain't goin' t' do now, an' what some other folks might do, is two different things. Ah tell ye it ain't safe fer ye t' stay up here in these hills at all."

"Listen to me, Thompson. I don't know who this man is that looks like me, but

I have every reason to believe that my name is Wingate. The record in the family Bible at home says I am, and what I read in that book I believe. You're wrong, Buddy. I am Wingate. I was a lieutenant in the flying corps during the war with Germany. These young women were over there too, as nurses, ambulance drivers and in other wartime occupations. When we returned to the United States, we decided to take a vacation in the saddle each season until we tired of it. The first season we rode over the Apache Trail in Arizona. Last year we crossed the Great American Desert in the west. This season we decided to come up here and combine business with pleasure."

Thompson's under jaw, Hippy observed, was sagging a little.

"An uncle, among other things, left me some mountain property on White River Ridge. I have never seen it, but I am now on my way to look it over and see if it is worth anything. That is the business to which I referred, and is the only business I have in the Kentucky mountains. Are you satisfied?"

"If Ah ain't, Ah'll give you-all warnin' that somebody'll shoot ye till you-all's daid!" warned Jed Thompson.

"That is a game two can play at. I have played at it myself," chuckled Lieutenant Wingate. "You have given me a timely warning, and I'll return the compliment, old dear."

"What's that ye say?"

"I have not said it; I am about to say it. Listen, Jed! Bat Spurgeon's gang has planned to come over here on the twenty-third and shoot up you and your crowd until you-all are 'daid,'" was Hippy Wingate's solemn warning. "Put that in your pipe and smoke it."

# CHAPTER XXII
# JULIE BRINGS DISTURBING NEWS

I s that right, Loot'nant?" demanded the mountaineer, leaning forward and peering searchingly at his informant.

"It is my information."

"Whar you hear it?"

"I overheard it one night. Another thing. That friend of yours, Lum Bangs, I should not trust too far were I in your place. Mind you, I don't speak with any knowledge that he isn't your friend, but I should advise you to keep your eyes on him."

"Ah reckons you-all ain't such a fool as ye look," grunted Jed Thompson, turning abruptly and striding away.

"Whew! That was a blow below the belt," muttered Hippy. "I am glad that Emma Dean didn't hear that."

Lieutenant Wingate heard Thompson getting his horse from the barn, and, a moment or so later, saw him riding away, rifle thrust in the saddle boot. Jed did not return until late that night, after all were asleep. The doctor had decided to remain all night with his patients, so Elfreda and Grace made up their beds in the barn for a much-needed night's rest.

Before they were awake next morning, the mountaineer had again ridden away, and soon after breakfast the girls began work on their equipment, patching up the tents and sewing the blankets that had been cut. The doctor reported that Lizzie and Sue were considerably improved, and decided that, if their improvement continued, he would return to Holcomb that afternoon.

This he did, leaving medicine and explicit directions after extracting a promise from the Overlanders to remain with the patients until he came up later in the week.

Three days later the Overland Riders, having finished their mending, pitched their camp in the open near the barn, where they felt much more comfortable.

During the days that followed the departure of the doctor, the girls and Julie came to know and understand each other better. Julie would sit for hours watching them at their sewing or knitting, as they in turn watched over the sick children. Elfreda told Julie of their work in France, of the bravery of Grace Harlowe and Hippy Wingate; of the little orphan that Grace had taken from a deserted French village one night and later adopted; of her own little Lindy, the hermit's daughter, and of many other things that deeply interested the black-eyed, fiery mountain girl.

In return, however, Julie told very little of the affairs of the mountaineers. Like all of her kind she was close-mouthed, as the Kentucky mountain people had learned from bitter experience was the only way to safety, for an indiscreet word might be passed along and bring the revenue officers down on the moonshiners, which most of the mountain men were.

While nursing the sick girls, Grace wrote to Tom at Hall's Corners, asking him to wait there as the Overland outfit undoubtedly would be late in reaching the rendezvous. Hippy, in the meantime, with Julie's assistance, had found and bought a horse to take the place of his lost pony.

The doctor came up on Saturday, and after looking the patients over announced that they were now wholly out of danger.

"Then, I suppose we are no longer needed here," suggested Miss Briggs.

"Well, I shouldn't exactly say that, but it will be safe to leave them. Julie must have learned something from your attention to her sisters," said the doctor.

"She has learned to be helpful, at least," interjected Grace. "We would not go, but it is important that we start as soon as possible. However, Doctor, if you think we should stay longer, we will do so."

"Go on. You young women have done more than any one else has ever done for these people. Jed is a queer fellow, but I know he appreciates it, though he is diffident about saying so. Where is Jed, by the way?"

"We have seen him only once since you were here," Hippy informed him. "By the way, Doc, do you know a fellow named Jim Townsend?"

The doctor gave Lieutenant Wingate a quick, keen glance.

"Can't say as I ever met him," reflected the medical man, stroking his chin. "Why?"

Hippy shrugged his shoulders, but made no reply.

"Were I in your place, Lieutenant, I shouldn't mention that name up here. It might not be safe," he warned. The doctor changed the subject and began giving Julie explicit directions for the care of the sick children. Elfreda added some suggestions of her own regarding their food, which suggestions the doctor approved, and left after shaking hands and beaming upon each Overland Rider.

The next day being Sunday, the entire party rode to the little mountain church, three miles from the Thompson cabin, and attended services. The devoutness of these queer mountain folk, moonshiners and feudists included, interested them deeply.

Early the next morning, their equipment having already been packed, they bade good-bye to the Thompsons. Julie cried a little, and the sick children clung to Grace and Elfreda as if they could not let them go.

Before leaving, Nora slipped some money into Julie's hand.

"This is for new clothes and shoes for yourself, the children and your mother," she whispered. "My Hippy wished me to give it to you." Giving Julie an impulsive kiss, Nora ran out without giving the mountain girl opportunity to recover from her surprise, and, after Julie had recovered, her amazement at the amount of money held in her hand left her altogether speechless until the Overland Riders had jogged away and were out of sight.

They were short on equipment and provisions, but knew that they could replenish their supplies at the general store at Hall's Corners.

Although they might have made the journey in two days' hard riding, it was decided to make camp early in the afternoon and rest up and enjoy the scenery, and on the following day camp about five miles from their destination, going on to Hall's Corners on the third day. After their idleness at Thompson's all hands were thoroughly enjoying being back in the saddle, and even Emma was enjoying herself so keenly that she forgot to be petulant or to "con-centrate" on anything at all.

In the two days' ride, which they made without incident, meeting very few persons, and not being annoyed by any one, they had come to hope that they had left the troubled area of the mountains behind them and that only peaceful scenes lay before them. Hippy, however, still insisted that he was a marked man.

It was some time after the evening meal of the second day when they heard a horse galloping along the wagon trail that they had followed ever since leaving the Thompson place.

Hippy held up a hand for silence, and the Overlanders sat listening intently.

"Some one is in an awful hurry," observed Emma.

"Going for a doctor, perhaps," suggested Hippy. "That's the way I rode when I went after old Doc Weatherby."

"Only one rider," announced Grace. "Otherwise we might have reason to feel disturbed."

The horse suddenly slowed down, its rider probably attracted by the light of the campfire.

"Hulloa the camp!" shouted a voice.

"A woman!" exclaimed Nora.

"Hulloa! Come on in so we can see who you are," called Emma.

"Howdy," answered the rider, picking her way towards them from the trail.

"Julie!" cried the Overlanders, as Julie Thompson rode into the flickering light of the campfire.

"What is the matter? Has something gone wrong, Julie?" begged Grace, running forward, her companions following close at her heels.

"Ah reckons somethin' is goin' t' right smart," answered the girl, slowly dismounting.

Washington was summoned to take her horse, with directions to water and groom it, for the animal was wet with sweat.

"See here! Where did you come from to-day?" demanded Hippy.

"Ah come from home, an' Ah been er ridin' ever since sunup, Ah have. Ah'm sore an' Ah'm hungry, folks!"

Nora and Anne ran to prepare food and coffee for their guest, while Grace and Elfreda led her to the fire and made Julie sit down.

"Is anything seriously wrong at home?" begged Miss Briggs.

Julie shook her head.

"Not yit. Thar may be. Liz an' Sue is feelin' fine. Paw ain't home, but he tole me t' find a hoss an' git to you-all as fast as Ah could. Ah didn't have no horse so Ah helped mahself t' one o' Lum Bangs' an' rid him right here."

They did not press Julie for the reason for her long hard ride until she had gulped down a cup of coffee, then Lieutenant Wingate suggested that she tell them what it was all about.

"Ah come t' warn you-all," she said. "Paw said as ye oughter know 'bout it right smart."

"Yes? What is it?" urged Grace.

"You-all got t' turn aroun' an' go back, 'cause Bat Spurgeon an' his gang is waitin' fer you-uns on the White River Ridge," announced Julie unemotionally.

Hippy uttered a partly suppressed whistle.

"That is where they are going to collect the price on your head," suggested Emma Dean.

"Sh--h--h!" rebuked Anne. "This is news to me. Who is Bat Spurgeon? Is there something you have kept back from us, Grace?"

"I don't know much about him except what Hippy told me after his capture by the mountaineers. I don't wish to speak of it here," with a significant glance at Julie. "How do you know this, Julie?" she asked, turning to the mountain girl.

"Paw! Don't know how Paw knowed 'bout it. Paw knows nigh everything 'bout what's doin' up here. Reckon you-all'll have er right smart time gittin' to the loot'nant's property ever, 'cause that's where Bat an' his bunch make their hang-out."

"Do they live there?" asked Hippy.

"Reckon they do now an' ag'in."

"They carry on their business there? Is that what you mean, Julie?" questioned Elfreda.

"Don't know nothin' 'bout that."

The girls exchanged significant glances. True to her type, Julie would not even expose an enemy. The Spurgeons and the Thompsons were feudists, and had time and again made war on each other for several generations, and it was their policy not to talk, but to let their rifles talk for them.

"What you-all goin' t' do?"

"We are going on, of course," announced Lieutenant Wingate.

"You-all shore'll git lammed if ye do," warned Julie.

"No we won't, 'cause I'll con-centrate. I think I will begin this very night, and by the time we reach that Ridge place all will be sweet peace," bubbled Emma.

Hippy Wingate shook his head and sighed.

"We must go as far as Hall's Corners, Julie. You know I have to meet my husband there. We shall, from then on, have one more man in the party and ought to be able to protect ourselves from those Spurgeon people," said Grace. "However, we will take up the question with Mr. Gray upon arrival at the Corners and decide upon what is best to be done."

"It is very fine of you, Julie," complimented Miss Briggs, laying a friendly hand on Julie's shoulder. "It really is wonderful that you should do all this for us."

"It has helped us a lot, Julie," added Anne. "You see we now know what to look out for. Otherwise we probably should have innocently walked right into trouble."

"And out again as fast as horseflesh could carry us," muttered Hippy. "What is your father going to do about the Spurgeons?"

"Ah don't know. 'Bout what?"

"Oh, most anything," answered Hippy lamely.

"Well, Ah reckon Ah'll be gittin' back home," sighed Julie.

"No, no!" protested the Overlanders in chorus. "You will remain here to-night. Your horse is tired out and so are you," added Grace.

It required considerable persuasion to induce the girl to stay, but she finally consented. Grace and Elfreda arranged to have Julie use their tent, for they wished to talk with her, and the result of that chat in the seclusion of the patched-up tent was that Grace and Elfreda gleaned considerable information. They learned from Julie, indirectly, that it was her father who sent Lum Bangs, in the guise of a game constable, to threaten the Overland party and drive them out of the mountains, her father having heard the story of the bear when he got home that day.

As to why Jed Thompson was so eager to be rid of the party, Julie had not a word to say, though her questioners had their own suspicions.

It was late when the three girls finally dropped off to sleep, but Julie was up with the break of day. Hearing her, Elfreda and Grace also got up and made a hurried breakfast, and assisted her in saddling her horse. Julie rode away waving her good-bye, happy in the thought of a good deed performed, for her brief association with the girls of the Overland party had opened her eyes to many things.

After breakfast the Overlanders held a consultation over what Julie had told them about conditions on White River Ridge, but deferred their decision as to what should be done until they had talked the situation over with Tom. Soon after that they packed up and rode away, reaching Hall's Corners about ten o'clock in the morning. They halted at the general store, which also was the post office, hitched their horses to the tie rail and hurried in for their mail.

"I have a letter from Tom," whispered Grace to Elfreda. "I must talk it over with the girls. Get them outside as soon as they can be induced to lay aside their letters."

"Not bad news, Loyalheart?"

"It may be," answered Grace. "Tom finished his government contract a week ago and went on to the Ridge to make the survey of Hippy's property before we got there, and leaves directions as to where we may find him. Elfreda, I don't like this at all."

"That means that we start for the Ridge and more trouble. Good! Let's go!"

## CHAPTER XXIII
## THE GATHERING OF THE CLANS

How long has Tom's letter been here?" asked Anne, after Grace had explained their situation to her companions.

"Ten days. Every one seems to be issuing warnings, and Tom is no exception. Listen to this, will you? 'Be vigilant! The white moonlight reigns supreme up here.'"

"What does he mean by that? Is Tom growing sentimental?" questioned Emma.

"He means there are moonshiners on this ridge of Lieutenant Wingate's," answered Miss Briggs.

"Huh! Brown Eyes, don't you worry about Tom. Any fellow who is slick enough to say a thing without saying it, is slick enough to outwit the whole breed of feudists and others up here."

Grace said she was not worrying, but that they must start as soon as they could replenish their stores. This they set about doing at once. New canvas with which to patch up their tents, cartridges for rifle and revolver, and provisions were purchased and lashed to the back of the remaining pack mule, or carried by the Overlanders in small packs on their ponies. As soon as possible, after studying the marked map that Tom Gray had left them to show the party where to look for his camp, they set out at a jog-trot, with which Washington and his mule had difficulty in keeping up.

That night they camped near the wagon trail, and at daylight resumed their journey. Late in the afternoon they halted for rest and to study their map and the contour of the mountains at that point.

"It should be somewhere hereabouts," declared Miss Briggs. "The landmarks appear to agree with Tom's markings on the map. It is my judgment that the wise thing to do would be to make camp near here."

After consultation it was decided to do this.

The part of the mountains where they were about to camp was the wildest and most rugged of any that they had seen since reaching Kentucky. Everywhere one saw caves, large and small, and unless one were vigilant he was quite likely to fall into one, for many were mere holes straight down through the rocks, and vine-covered at the top. The rocks themselves were misshapen, and in some instances hideous when the light of the day faded.

"Hippy, is this your property?" questioned Emma as they sat down to their supper.

"Yes. Why?"

"You ought to come and spend the rest of your days here. What a lovely spot over on that knoll for a bungalow. I think--"

A distant rifle shot interrupted what Emma was about to say. It was followed by several others in quick succession, but, while apparently not very far away, no bullets were heard, so the Overland Riders felt that they were not the object of the shooting.

"Beginning already," muttered Elfreda.

Grace said nothing. She was listening and wondering if Tom were out there, and if so, if he were in trouble. However, there was nothing to be done except to wait until morning before pushing their search for him further. The camp was well guarded that night, but nothing occurred to disturb them.

Shortly after daylight a systematic search was begun for Tom Gray's camp, the Overlanders separating and going out for individual search, keeping the landmarks near their own camp well in mind.

It was Elfreda Briggs who made the discovery. She called to Grace, who was near by, to come to her. Grace uttered an exclamation as she ran up to Miss Briggs, who stood pointing to a little tent nestling at the base of a rocky peak.

"Is that Tom's tent?" asked Elfreda.

"No, but we will have a look at it."

The two girls ran eagerly to the little tent, proceeding more cautiously as they came up to it. The blankets, they found, were rolled neatly, and a pair of boots stood in one corner, while some clothing hung from hooks on a tent-pole.

"This *is* Tom's tent. Oh, I am so glad," cried Grace.

"Yes. But where is Tom?"

"It is all right. He may be away from here for days, sleeping in the open, living as only a woodsman knows how to live. You know he is making a survey of this tract, and, I presume, doesn't find it convenient to take his equipment with him. Now I am content to settle down and wait for him. In the meantime we can do some exploring on our own account. I wonder who Tom has with him?"

"What do you mean?"

"Tracks of two different persons right there," answered Grace, pointing to the ground. "Where are your eyes, J. Elfreda?"

"Let's go back," suggested Miss Briggs, sighing deeply. "We must let the girls know at once."

All the Overlanders, except Nora Wingate, were quickly rounded up and told the good news. Nora was nowhere in sight, but Hippy said she was picking mountain berries about a quarter of a mile to the south of the camp, and that she had probably forgotten what she had been sent out for. He said, however, that he would go out and look for her.

In the meantime, Nora had been sitting eating the hatful of berries that she had gathered, gazing off over the rugged landscape and enjoying the mountain scenery bathed in the early morning sunlight. The mountains, in that softening light, lost their hideousness and were really beautiful to look upon. Nora's eyes, slowly absorbing the scene before her, suddenly paused in their roving and fixed their gaze on a point some twenty yards below her. Nora was looking down on the crown of a sombrero. Below it, the figure that the hat belonged to was invisible in the dense growth of vine and bush.

"Faith, and what's that?" murmured Nora, half humorously. "I know. It's that husband of mine wanting to give me a scare. Wait! I'll make the rascal jump."

Nora Wingate groped for and found a small piece of rock, chuckling softly to herself. Rising cautiously she aimed the rock to fall several feet to one side of the man below her, then reaching her hand far back she let fly, just as she had seen bombers do in France when practicing bomb-throwing.

Nora stood shaking with silent laughter at the fright she was going to give Hippy Wingate. To her horror, the rock, instead of landing to one side of the man, dropped fairly on the top of his head. As the stone hit him, the man uttered a grunt, but the Overland girl was too shocked to utter a sound.

The fellow leaped to one side, threw a hand to his head and knocked off his hat in his effort to find out what had hit him, then quickly looked up.

Nora Wingate found herself gazing down, not into the face of Hippy, but into the scowling, rage-contorted features of Lum Bangs. At that moment, Nora, of her own volition, could not have moved to save her life, but Lum speedily furnished the incentive for her to do so. Without an instant's hesitation he fired his rifle from the hip. The bullet from it cut the leaves not many inches from Nora's head.

"Hippy! Oh, Hippy!" she screamed and ran, bullets clipping the leaves close by, which served to lend speed to her flying feet.

Nora, as she ran, kept on shouting for Hippy. He heard her faintly and started at a run to meet her.

"They are shooting at me. Hurry! Run!" urged Nora as he neared her.

"Run? I guess not," retorted Hippy. "Where are they?"

"Up the mountain. There was only one, but there may be more." Nora grabbed her husband's arm and both started at a brisk trot for the camp. Reaching there, Nora hurriedly told her companions what had occurred.

"Lum Bangs!" exclaimed Miss Briggs. "What is he doing here? The Thompsons must be here."

Grace shook her head and said she doubted it.

"Julie warned us against the Spurgeons and said they were waiting for us on this ridge," reminded Grace. "Still, that doesn't explain Lum's presence here, unless he has followed us, seeking revenge."

"Lum may have turned traitor," observed Hippy. "Folks, it is my opinion that we had better prepare for trouble. I smell it in the air."

"Don't you think that it would be wise to protect our equipment?" suggested Anne.

Grace pondered, then announced that for the present they would do nothing beyond looking for a place not only to stow their belongings, but to safeguard themselves in case of trouble. They found such a place in a cave that Hippy had discovered that morning, the opening to which was on a slight rise of ground, commanding a wide view across the valley below it.

The party investigated the cave, and, finding it suited to their needs, began to move into it. Tents, mess kits, some food and a few blankets were all that were left in the nearby camp. Hippy then assumed the duty of guarding the party, but not a sign of life did he discover, nor was there a disturbing sound to be heard. Supper was eaten in camp before dark and the cook fire then extinguished.

Grace was troubled about Tom, and, as the hours wore on, the thought that perhaps he might have come to some harm, grew upon her. She got up about midnight, and, leaving her tent, sat down on a rock, chin in hands, more nervous than she remembered ever to have been before. Hurried footsteps aroused her to instant alertness.

"Is that you, Hippy?" called a low-pitched voice off to the right of her. It was Nora Wingate's voice. Grace had not known she was awake.

"Yes. Wake the girls, but be quiet about it. The woods are full of them."

"Of whom?" demanded Grace, getting quickly to her feet and hurrying to Hippy.

"I don't know, but I saw several men about two hundred yards from here. They are creeping up on the camp. Hurry! Get the girls into the cave. I will keep watch here until you get safely to the cave."

It was but a few minutes later when the Overland girls filed silently from their camp and headed for the cave. Hippy, rifle in hand, halted just outside the camp and waited. He did not have long to wait. A burst of rifle fire woke the mountain echoes, but, being out of the range of fire, he merely crouched down and waited to see what the attackers would do.

In the cave, the Overland girls were peering from the opening, but, by agreement, not a shot was fired by them or by Lieutenant Wingate.

The shooting kept up briskly for several minutes, then died away, and silence settled over the scene. Hippy remained near the camp so long that the girls began to feel concerned for him. This was dispelled nearly half an hour later when they discovered him, well bent over to hide his movements, running towards them.

"Whew! They didn't do a thing to our tents. Shot them full of holes," he exclaimed. "They are going through everything and they're getting worried, judging from what I overheard. We played a neat trick on them," chuckled the lieutenant.

"Don't crow," advised Emma Dean. "It isn't daylight yet. I will con-centrate. I con-centrated all the time you were away, and you came back, didn't you?"

"'Con-centrate' on those ruffians and drive them away; 'con-centrate' on Tom Gray; 'con-centrate' on the Mystery Man--'con-centrate' on anybody, but for the love of Mike don't let loose any of that 'imponderable quantity' on me," begged Lieutenant Wingate.

Hippy advised the girls to lie down on their blankets and try to sleep, saying that he would keep awake and watch at the cave entrance, but none of them felt the slightest desire for sleep, especially when the rifle fire opened up again. They wondered if the attackers were shooting at shadows. Not more than a dozen shots were fired and these at intervals, after which there was no more shooting during the rest of the night.

At daybreak Hippy dozed off, first nodding to Nora to take the watch for him, which she did. The others of the party were sitting on the rocky floor of the cave leaning against the wall, also dozing. Nora, for a short time, sat watching her husband who was snoring loudly; then she got up and peered out at the reddening sky. Unthinkingly, she stepped from the cave and stood inhaling deeply of the fragrant morning air.

Nora suddenly uttered a cry and clapped a hand to her left cheek. At the same instant, it seemed, the report of a rifle woke the echoes.

Hippy, awake and on his feet in an instant, jerked Nora back into the cave, but not before a bullet had flattened itself against the rocks close to his head.

"Lie down and keep tight to the sides of the cave!" he commanded. "They know where we are now. Fine! Fine! Emma Dean could do no worse."

No more shots were fired for fully an hour, then suddenly bullets began to pour into the cave, some hitting the sides and, ricochetting, wailed on into the dark depths of the cavern, making any part of the gloomy place unsafe. The best the Overlanders could do was to keep down and lie close to the wall.

Nora had had a narrow escape from death at the first shot, though, while she had not been hit, the bullet had grazed her cheek, leaving a red mark across it.

Frequent volleys into the cave, after several hours, set the nerves of each of the Overland Riders on edge. Hippy was eager to take a hand in the fray, but the girls forbade it, advising him that he would merely be making a mark of himself, whereas it were doubtful if he could see a single one of their assailants.

"Yes, but suppose they keep us here for days?" objected Lieutenant Wingate.

"We have plenty of food," answered Anne.

"And precious little water," added Grace Harlowe. "My advice is to wait and watch. At night they are certain to come up closer to the mouth of the cave. Perhaps we may be able to get a shot at them then without exposing ourselves. Surely, if they try to enter here we can quickly drive them back."

The rest of the afternoon up to three o'clock was spent in dodging bullets. Exactly on the hour of three there came an interruption that startled every one of the cave dwellers. A rattling fire sprang up, but no bullets came their way. Hippy held up his hand for silence, and listened.

"Two gangs are at it and they must be shooting at each other. I'm going out to have a look!" cried Hippy.

"Look! Look!" cried Emma, whose curiosity had led her to follow Lieutenant Wingate.

Men were seen running down below them. On the opposite mountainside, just across the narrow valley that lay a short distance from the mouth of the cave, they saw skulking figures. Now and then one would drop to his knees and shoot at the fleeing figures in the valley.

The fleeing men in the valley, after reaching the positions they were seeking, faced their adversaries on the mountainside and began firing up at them.

"It is the feud!" cried Miss Briggs.

"That's right. I have it!" exclaimed Hippy. "This is the twenty-second of the month. The Spurgeons were going to sail into the Thompsons on the twenty-third, but Jed Thompson has beat them to it by a day, and attacked them on the twenty-second. Good generalship!"

"I call it terrible," murmured Anne Nesbit.

From their elevated position, the Overland Riders were able to observe the battle in all its details, and it was a thrilling sight. They saw men fall, but whether from bullet or from stumbling the Overlanders did not know, for, in most instances, the fallen ones soon got to their feet and joined in the fight. Now and then, however, one remained where he had dropped.

"I think the party on the mountainside is the Thompson party," announced Grace, who had been observing through her binoculars. "I am positive that I recognize Jed."

"Then the Spurgeons are on the run. Look at that, will you!" cried Lieutenant Wingate.

The supposed Spurgeons were now dashing down the valley, here and there making a stand and shooting up at their enemies, who were pouring down a hot fire on them. The shooting soon began to die down, with an occasional shot from the Thompson feudists, probably long-range shots at the fleeing figures of the Spurgeons.

"All over," announced Hippy. "We can now safely go out. I am going over to see what the camp looks like."

The girls said they too would go. They did not believe that their presence had been discovered by the Thompson fighters, but in this, however, they were mistaken. Keen eyes had espied them watching the battle from the mouth of the cave, and even then some of the Thompson party was on its way to look the Overlanders over.

Washington Washington, who, during the firing on the cave, had remained flat on his stomach on the floor, a finger in either ear, trembling with fright, now assured that he had nothing more to fear, darted on ahead, eager to get to his mule. He gained the camp a few minutes ahead of the Overland party. They saw him coming back, wide-eyed, his feet barely touching the ground as he ran.

"What is it, Laundry?" called Hippy.

Washington's lips refused to frame the words that he was trying to utter. The Overlanders started forward at a run, bringing up abruptly as they gained their camping place. Not a vestige of it, save the ashes of their cook fire, remained. Everything was gone.

"De hosses!" exploded Washington.

"They're gone!" cried Emma Dean, who, following Washington's warning, had run to the tethering place.

They were not all "gone," however. The Overland Riders found that one pony had been, shot through the head, and that the mule had shared a like fate. The other animals had disappeared, probably driven away by Bat Spurgeon and his gang of ruffians.

"Howd', folks," greeted Jed Thompson, fairly bursting into the camp. "You-all don't know whether that critter Spurgeon has been heyeh, does ye?"

"Just cast your eagle eyes about and see if you don't think it looks as if some-body had been here, old top," answered Hippy Wingate, taking in the camp and the tethering ground with a wave of the hand.

"Our ponies are gone. Now we've got to walk all the way home," wailed Emma.

"'Con-centrate,' little one," advised Hippy.

"Never mind 'bout the hosses. We-uns'll fix ye up. Spurgeon and Lum Bates got er-way. They come this-a-way an' Ah reckon they're hidin' in a cave. Shore they ain't in that place where you was?" demanded Jed.

"If ye ain't sartin, better look an' see. We'll be goin' through t'other holes right smart. Mah men is doin' it now!"

"Bates?" wondered Hippy.

"The houn' went back on we-uns. It was this-a-way. Lum opined as we ought ter follow ye and clean yer outfit up, but Ah said as after you-uns had done what you-all had done fer Liz an' Sue, there wan't nothin' doin'. That was the last Ah seen of the houn' dawg. Ah know he was with Spurgeon 'cause Ah put er bullet through his shoulder ter-day."

"Sorry I couldn't have had a crack at him myself," muttered Hippy.

"It was Lum that pestered ye so. Ah set him on ye an' put up that bear story, but you-all didn't swaller it," he added, nodding to Hippy. "Say, Loot'nant, are ye sartin you-all ain't Jim Townsend?"

"Well," reflected Hippy, "I may say I am reasonably certain that I'm not."

"You folks wait here till we-uns come back. Mebby 'twon't be till mornin', fer we've got t' git that houn', Lum, an' Bat Spurgeon, else they won't be no livin' round heyeh. This yer property?" with a sweeping wave of the hand.

Hippy nodded.

"Good thing we-uns cleaned out the Spurgeons then. Won't be none o' 'em 'round when you moves up heyeh. Bye." And Jed left them at a trot.

"I am going to investigate our cave. You can come along if you want to, but if that fellow with the explosive name-- *Bangs*--should chance to be there I'll tell you in advance you better make tracks lively, for there surely will be some shooting," warned Hippy.

Torches were prepared and Washington reluctantly led the way into the cave with one, Hippy walking behind him with drawn revolver, the Overland girls bringing up the rear a few yards from Lieutenant Wingate.

Not having explored the cave very far, they were amazed at its depth; in fact they had gone on, it seemed, a good mile and were still looking for the end.

"I don't believe there is any one in here," Hippy was saying. "We might as well go back."

"Ahem!"

"Who said that?" demanded Hippy.

"Ahem!"

Washington Washington uttered a yell and bolted back for the opening of the cave, taking his torch with him, leaving the Overlanders in the blackest darkness they had ever experienced.

"I make the near blind to see, and the seeing to see in the dark as in the daylight. I am the benefactor of all-uns of the mountains. Specs, ladies and gentlemen--fit you with specs that will enable you to penetrate even the darkness of the under-earth. Nick-nacks, threads, needles, but principally specs and good cheer," announced a voice that seemed to come right up out of the earth before them.

# CHAPTER XXIV
# TRAIL'S END

The Mystery Man!" shouted the Overland Riders.

"Oh, Mr. Long, where are you?" cried Grace.

"I am here, bound over to keep the peace. If you will kindly release me I will stretch myself, fit you with specs and proceed to break the peace as soon as I can catch sight of the fellows who put me here. Specs, folks? If you cannot wait, fetch my case. It is here somewhere, and I'll fit you before you untie me."

Hippy struck a match, and by its light they saw Jeremiah Long, arms pinioned to his sides with rope, and a rope about his neck, fastened to a stake driven into a crevice in the rocks.

The Mystery Man was quickly released.

"Do you not wish to hear what has occurred here?" asked Nora.

"Ah know what occurred, up to the time some one hit me over the head and put me to sleep."

Hippy then briefly told him the story of their arrival at the Ridge, and of what followed. Grace added that they were disturbed, very much worried about Tom Gray, and asked Mr. Long if he would assist them in finding him.

"To be sure. Here! Place these specs on your nose and I promise you that through those magic lenses you shall see your husband this very night. Do they fit you?" questioned Jeremiah Long.

"The bows fit perfectly, but I cannot see a thing through the lenses," answered Grace laughingly, as a match flared up in the hands of Nora Wingate and was held before Grace Harlowe's face.

"That is as it should be. So long as the bows fit, it matters not about the lenses. Hold your positions, please, and light no matches until I tell you to, lest you destroy the magic spell."

The Mystery Man left them, but returned in a few moments.

"I will throw a gleam from my magic lamp, and through your magic lenses, Mrs. Gray, you will see that my spell has worked," announced the strange character. He flashed an electric pocket lamp on the face of a man standing facing the party.

The Overlanders gasped.

The circle of light drew the face of Tom Gray out of the darkness.

"Tom!" cried Grace, snatching off the spectacles and running to her husband. "Oh, Tom, how could you keep silent so long when you knew how disturbed we were?"

"I could not well do otherwise, Grace, seeing that I was bound just as Mr. Long was, but with the added burden of a gag in my mouth. He came in after I did, and we managed to get acquainted despite my gag. I could mumble and he got the mumble. After you released him he freed my mouth of the gag and cut the rope that held me helpless."

"You see my magic specs saw that Captain Gray had been clubbed and kidnapped, and I was trying to find him when I was put to sleep and dumped in here to await further disposition. Have the specs fulfilled all that I promised, Mrs. Gray?"

"A hundred fold," laughed Grace happily.

"No charge, thank you. We aim to please our customers. Having an appointment late this evening to fit a pair of specs of another variety than you have seen me display, I will bid you good-evening. If I do not see you again in reality, I shall many times smile at you ladies with my eyes and my heart, and, should you at such times chance to be wearing the magic specs, you will see the smile and recall the smiler."

"Won't you shake hands?" asked Miss Briggs.

"Thank you. I have said my good-byes."

"At least, Mr. Long, before you leave us, please tell us who and what you are," urged Nora.

"With pleasure. I am Jeremiah Long, the Mystery Man, and spectacles is my line. All hay is grass and grass is hay. I'm here to-morrow and gone to-day." His voice seemed to fade away in the darkness, the last words sounding far away and barely heard. The Overland Riders did not know whether he had gone out or plunged deeper into the cave, to emerge from some exit the existence of which they were unaware.

"What a queer man," murmured Anne Nesbit. "He almost gives one the creeps. I wish we knew who and what he is."

"I think Tom knows," spoke up Grace. "Let's get out of this horrid place."

"Yes, I do know. To-night he expects to accomplish what he has been working towards for many months, a round-up of the leading moonshiners of this district. I have seen Long before I came up here, and he confided in me, because I possessed some information, gleaned from hiking over this property of yours, which he wished to have, and that he could not very well ask for without giving me some information in return. Long is Dick Whitfield, the head of a corps of mountain sleuths, probably the shrewdest man in his line of work who ever came into the Kentucky hills. It was he who wounded the mountaineer in the bushes that night by your camp. It was he who protected you in many tight places, including some that you did not know about."

"And shot Lum Bangs through the wrist at the dance," suggested Nora.

"No, that was Jim Townsend, his principal assistant."

"That's the fellow I want to know about--the fellow who ought to be the proudest man in the world because he looks like me," cried Hippy Wingate.

As the party strolled out towards the mouth of the tunnel, Tom Gray told his companions that Hippy's resemblance to Townsend had been quickly seized upon by the Mystery Man, Jeremiah Long, and used as a cloak to cover the operations of the real Townsend, trusting to their skill and watchfulness to keep the moonshiners from collecting the reward that had been offered for Townsend. Either Townsend or the Spectacle Man had kept the Overland Riders under observation a good part of the time. It was Townsend who rescued Hippy from the Spurgeon gang, who conducted Hippy back to his camp, and who left the mysterious notes for the Overlanders.

"Yes. But why did they mark me for the slaughter?" demanded Hippy.

"Don't you understand? They thought you were Jim Townsend. In fact, the mountain men had been informed that Townsend was on his way here as a member of the Overland Riders, to get evidence against the moonshiners. As a matter of fact, Townsend was already here and had been, in disguise, for some time. That belief involved our entire party, you see, and it is a wonder that the mountaineers did not get one of you, at least. When they caught me, knowing that I was in Government service, I thought it was all up with me, but I believe they thought best first to settle their feud with Thompson.

"One thing that possibly saved all of you people, and surely saved Hippy," resumed Tom Gray, "is that you are women. They were eager enough to put Hippy out of the way, but you girls made them hesitate. They didn't like the idea of committing a cold-blooded crime like that in the presence of a group of pretty girls."

"What about that survey you were to make for me?" questioned Hippy.

"I have made it," replied Tom. "That is, I have gone far enough with it to convince me that you have a wonderful coal deposit here. It will make you a richer man than you ever dreamed of being, but it will be at least two years before you can work the veins. A survey has been made for a railroad spur that will go through your property, and I believe the railroad people are going to begin work on it next spring. You will, therefore, have plenty of time to mature your plans for the big splash."

"Hippy Wingate, don't you dare go and get enlargement of the head," warned Nora, after his companions had crowded about Hippy and enthusiastically congratulated him.

"Never mind, Nora. If he does, just let me know. I'll con-centrate on his head until it gets so small that he can wear a charlotte russe cup on it instead of a sombrero. Didn't I con-centrate on everything?" demanded Emma triumphantly.

"You did," agreed Hippy in a guttural voice.

"And didn't everything turn out just as I con-centrated that it should?"

"It did," rumbled Hippy.

"Then there is nothing more to be said," finished Emma amid the laughter of her companions.

That night, having no tents to cover them, the Overland party slept in the cave. Tom Gray sat with Hippy on guard at the mouth of the cave all night, but their watchfulness was not needed. The Spurgeon gang that had been annoying them had been soundly whipped, and, one by one, those that were left were being arrested by revenue men. Spurgeon himself, as the Overlanders learned later, succeeded in getting away. Lum Bangs, too, managed to avoid the revenue agents, but was later hunted down and driven out of the mountains by Jed Thompson's friends.

Late on the morning following the fight, Jed and some of his men rode into the camp with the Overland ponies and also turned in one belonging to his own outfit to take the place of the animal that the Spurgeons had shot.

The Overland Riders spent a week longer in the mountains, during which Tom and Hippy went over the latter's property in detail and laid plans for the future.

Before leaving the mountains, Hippy succeeded in inducing Captain Gray to go into partnership with him and share in Hippy's good fortune. At the end of this happy week the Overlanders packed up what was left of their equipment and rode away towards home, stopping for a day for a visit with Jed Thompson's family, and incidentally to warn Jed that it might be wise for him to raise and use other crops than corn, lest the revenue men take him in as they had done with the Spurgeon gang.

In a way, the Overland girls were glad to start on their way home. None, however, was quite so happy to be homeward bound as was Washington Washington, who frankly admitted that he had had enough, and that he "didn' want no moah."

The further adventures of the Overland Riders will be related in a following volume entitled, "GRACE HARLOWE'S OVERLAND RIDERS IN THE GREAT NORTH WOODS." Battles with the timber pirates, the fight for the Overland claim, the faithfulness of the Indian, who helps Hippy and Tom on to victory, and the Christmas dinner in the depth of the forest amid thousands of scintillating Christmas trees, makes a story of adventure and achievement second to none that Grace Harlowe and her companions ever have experienced.

### The Codes Of Hammurabi And Moses
### W. W. Davies

QTY

The discovery of the Hammurabi Code is one of the greatest achievements of archaeology, and is of paramount interest, not only to the student of the Bible, but also to all those interested in ancient history...

**Religion**   **ISBN:** *1-59462-338-4*        **Pages:132**

*MSRP $12.95*

### The Theory of Moral Sentiments
### Adam Smith

QTY

This work from 1749. contains original theories of conscience amd moral judgment and it is the foundation for systemof morals.

**Philosophy**   **ISBN:** *1-59462-777-0*        **Pages:536**

*MSRP $19.95*

### Jessica's First Prayer
### Hesba Stretton

QTY

In a screened and secluded corner of one of the many railway-bridges which span the streets of London there could be seen a few years ago, from five o'clock every morning until half past eight, a tidily set-out coffee-stall, consisting of a trestle and board, upon which stood two large tin cans, with a small fire of charcoal burning under each so as to keep the coffee boiling during the early hours of the morning when the work-people were thronging into the city on their way to their daily toil...

**Pages:84**

**Childrens**   **ISBN:** *1-59462-373-2*     *MSRP $9.95*

### My Life and Work
### Henry Ford

QTY

Henry Ford revolutionized the world with his implementation of mass production for the Model T automobile. Gain valuable business insight into his life and work with his own auto-biography... "We have only started on our development of our country we have not as yet, with all our talk of wonderful progress, done more than scratch the surface. The progress has been wonderful enough but..."

**Pages:300**

**Biographies/**   **ISBN:** *1-59462-198-5*     *MSRP $21.95*

## The Art of Cross-Examination
## Francis Wellman

QTY

I presume it is the experience of every author, after his first book is published upon an important subject, to be almost overwhelmed with a wealth of ideas and illustrations which could readily have been included in his book, and which to his own mind, at least, seem to make a second edition inevitable. Such certainly was the case with me; and when the first edition had reached its sixth impression in five months, I rejoiced to learn that it seemed to my publishers that the book had met with a sufficiently favorable reception to justify a second and considerably enlarged edition. ...

**Pages:412**

**Reference**   **ISBN:** *1-59462-647-2*       *MSRP $19.95*

## On the Duty of Civil Disobedience
## Henry David Thoreau

QTY

Thoreau wrote his famous essay, On the Duty of Civil Disobedience, as a protest against an unjust but popular war and the immoral but popular institution of slave-owning. He did more than write—he declined to pay his taxes, and was hauled off to gaol in consequence. Who can say how much this refusal of his hastened the end of the war and of slavery ?

**Law**       **ISBN:** *1-59462-747-9*       **Pages:48**

*MSRP $7.45*

## Dream Psychology Psychoanalysis for Beginners
## Sigmund Freud

QTY

Sigmund Freud, born Sigismund Schlomo Freud (May 6, 1856 - September 23, 1939), was a Jewish-Austrian neurologist and psychiatrist who co-founded the psychoanalytic school of psychology. Freud is best known for his theories of the unconscious mind, especially involving the mechanism of repression; his redefinition of sexual desire as mobile and directed towards a wide variety of objects; and his therapeutic techniques, especially his understanding of transference in the therapeutic relationship and the presumed value of dreams as sources of insight into unconscious desires.

Dream Psychology
Psychoanalysis for Beginners

Sigmund Freud

**Pages:196**

**Psychology**   **ISBN:** *1-59462-905-6*       *MSRP $15.45*

## The Miracle of Right Thought
## Orison Swett Marden

QTY

Believe with all of your heart that you will do what you were made to do. When the mind has once formed the habit of holding cheerful, happy, prosperous pictures, it will not be easy to form the opposite habit. It does not matter how improbable or how far away this realization may see, or how dark the prospects may be, if we visualize them as best we can, as vividly as possible, hold tenaciously to them and vigorously struggle to attain them, they will gradually become actualized, realized in the life. But a desire, a longing without endeavor, a yearning abandoned or held indifferently will vanish without realization.

**Pages:360**

**Self Help**       **ISBN:** *1-59462-644-8*       *MSRP $25.45*

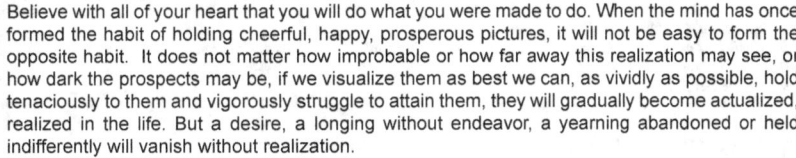

**www.bookjungle.com** *email: sales@bookjungle.com fax: 630-214-0564 mail: Book Jungle PO Box 2226 Champaign, IL 61825*

QTY

**The Rosicrucian Cosmo-Conception Mystic Christianity** *by Max Heindel*  ISBN: *1-59462-188-8*  **$38.95**
*The Rosicrucian Cosmo-conception is not dogmatic, neither does it appeal to any other authority than the reason of the student. It is: not controversial, but is: sent forth in the, hope that it may help to clear...*  New Age/Religion Pages 646

**Abandonment To Divine Providence** *by Jean-Pierre de Caussade*  ISBN: *1-59462-228-0*  **$25.95**
*"The Rev. Jean Pierre de Caussade was one of the most remarkable spiritual writers of the Society of Jesus in France in the 18th Century. His death took place at Toulouse in 1751. His works have gone through many editions and have been republished...*  Inspirational/Religion Pages 400

**Mental Chemistry** *by Charles Haanel*  ISBN: *1-59462-192-6*  **$23.95**
*Mental Chemistry allows the change of material conditions by combining and appropriately utilizing the power of the mind. Much like applied chemistry creates something new and unique out of careful combinations of chemicals the mastery of mental chemistry...*  New Age Pages 354

**The Letters of Robert Browning and Elizabeth Barret Barrett 1845-1846 vol II**  ISBN: *1-59462-193-4*  **$35.95**
*by Robert Browning and Elizabeth Barrett*  Biographies Pages 596

**Gleanings In Genesis (volume I)** *by Arthur W. Pink*  ISBN: *1-59462-130-6*  **$27.45**
*Appropriately has Genesis been termed "the seed plot of the Bible" for in it we have, in germ form, almost all of the great doctrines which are afterwards fully developed in the books of Scripture which follow...*  Religion/Inspirational Pages 420

**The Master Key** *by L. W. de Laurence*  ISBN: *1-59462-001-6*  **$30.95**
*In no branch of human knowledge has there been a more lively increase of the spirit of research during the past few years than in the study of Psychology, Concentration and Mental Discipline. The requests for authentic lessons in Thought Control, Mental Discipline and...*  New Age/Business Pages 422

**The Lesser Key Of Solomon Goetia** *by L. W. de Laurence*  ISBN: *1-59462-092-X*  **$9.95**
*This translation of the first book of the "Lemegton" which is now for the first time made accessible to students of Talismanic Magic was done, after careful collation and edition, from numerous Ancient Manuscripts in Hebrew, Latin, and French...*  New Age/Occult Pages 92

**Rubaiyat Of Omar Khayyam** *by Edward Fitzgerald*  ISBN:*1-59462-332-5*  **$13.95**
*Edward Fitzgerald, whom the world has already learned, in spite of his own efforts to remain within the shadow of anonymity, to look upon as one of the rarest poets of the century, was born at Bredfield, in Suffolk, on the 31st of March, 1809. He was the third son of John Purcell...*  Music Pages 172

**Ancient Law** *by Henry Maine*  ISBN: *1-59462-128-4*  **$29.95**
*The chief object of the following pages is to indicate some of the earliest ideas of mankind, as they are reflected in Ancient Law, and to point out the relation of those ideas to modern thought.*  Religion/History Pages 452

**Far-Away Stories** *by William J. Locke*  ISBN: *1-59462-129-2*  **$19.45**
*"Good wine needs no bush, but a collection of mixed vintages does. And this book is just such a collection. Some of the stories I do not want to remain buried for ever in the museum files of dead magazine-numbers an author's not unpardonable vanity..."*  Fiction Pages 272

**Life of David Crockett** *by David Crockett*  ISBN: *1-59462-250-7*  **$27.45**
*"Colonel David Crockett was one of the most remarkable men of the times in which he lived. Born in humble life, but gifted with a strong will, an indomitable courage, and unremitting perseverance...*  Biographies/New Age Pages 424

**Lip-Reading** *by Edward Nitchie*  ISBN: *1-59462-206-X*  **$25.95**
*Edward B. Nitchie, founder of the New York School for the Hard of Hearing, now the Nitchie School of Lip-Reading, Inc, wrote "LIP-READING Principles and Practice". The development and perfecting of this meritorious work on lip-reading was an undertaking...*  How-to Pages 400

**A Handbook of Suggestive Therapeutics, Applied Hypnotism, Psychic Science**  ISBN: *1-59462-214-0*  **$24.95**
*by Henry Munro*  Health/New Age/Health/Self-help Pages 376

**A Doll's House: and Two Other Plays** *by Henrik Ibsen*  ISBN: *1-59462-112-8*  **$19.95**
*Henrik Ibsen created this classic when in revolutionary 1848 Rome. Introducing some striking concepts in playwriting for the realist genre, this play has been studied the world over.*  Fiction/Classics/Plays 308

**The Light of Asia** *by sir Edwin Arnold*  ISBN: *1-59462-204-3*  **$13.95**
*In this poetic masterpiece, Edwin Arnold describes the life and teachings of Buddha. The man who was to become known as Buddha to the world was born as Prince Gautama of India but he rejected the worldly riches and abandoned the reigns of power when...*  Religion/History/Biographies Pages 170

**The Complete Works of Guy de Maupassant** *by Guy de Maupassant*  ISBN: *1-59462-157-8*  **$16.95**
*"For days and days, nights and nights, I had dreamed of that first kiss which was to consecrate our engagement, and I knew not on what spot I should put my lips..."*  Fiction/Classics Pages 240

**The Art of Cross-Examination** *by Francis L. Wellman*  ISBN: *1-59462-309-0*  **$26.95**
*Written by a renowned trial lawyer, Wellman imparts his experience and uses case studies to explain how to use psychology to extract desired information through questioning.*  How-to/Science/Reference Pages 408

**Answered or Unanswered?** *by Louisa Vaughan*  ISBN: *1-59462-248-5*  **$10.95**
*Miracles of Faith in China*  Religion Pages 112

**The Edinburgh Lectures on Mental Science (1909)** *by Thomas*  ISBN: *1-59462-008-3*  **$11.95**
*This book contains the substance of a course of lectures recently given by the writer in the Queen Street Hall, Edinburgh. Its purpose is to indicate the Natural Principles governing the relation between Mental Action and Material Conditions...*  New Age/Psychology Pages 148

**Ayesha** *by H. Rider Haggard*  ISBN: *1-59462-301-5*  **$24.95**
*Verily and indeed it is the unexpected that happens! Probably if there was one person upon the earth from whom the Editor of this, and of a certain previous history, did not expect to hear again...*  Classics Pages 380

**Ayala's Angel** *by Anthony Trollope*  ISBN: *1-59462-352-X*  **$29.95**
*The two girls were both pretty, but Lucy who was twenty-one who supposed to be simple and comparatively unattractive, whereas Ayala was credited, as her Bombwhat romantic name might show, with poetic charm and a taste for romance. Ayala when her father died was nineteen...*  Fiction Pages 484

**The American Commonwealth** *by James Bryce*  ISBN: *1-59462-286-8*  **$34.45**
*An interpretation of American democratic political theory. It examines political mechanics and society from the perspective of Scotsman James Bryce*  Politics Pages 572

**Stories of the Pilgrims** *by Margaret P. Pumphrey*  ISBN: *1-59462-116-0*  **$17.95**
*This book explores pilgrims religious oppression in England as well as their escape to Holland and eventual crossing to America on the Mayflower, and their early days in New England...*  History Pages 268

www.bookjungle.com *email: sales@bookjungle.com fax: 630-214-0564 mail: Book Jungle  PO Box 2226  Champaign, IL 61825*

**QTY**

**The Fasting Cure** *by Sinclair Upton*　　　　　　　　ISBN: *1-59462-222-1*　**$13.95**
*In the Cosmopolitan Magazine for May, 1910, and in the Contemporary Review (London) for April, 1910, I published an article dealing with my experiences in fasting. I have written a great many magazine articles, but never one which attracted so much attention...* New Age/Self Help/Health Pages 164

**Hebrew Astrology** *by Sepharial*　　　　　　　　ISBN: *1-59462-308-2*　**$13.45**
*In these days of advanced thinking it is a matter of common observation that we have left many of the old landmarks behind and that we are now pressing forward to greater heights and to a wider horizon than that which represented the mind-content of our progenitors...* Astrology Pages 144

**Thought Vibration or The Law of Attraction in the Thought World**　ISBN: *1-59462-127-6*　**$12.95**
*by William Walker Atkinson*　　　　　　　　Psychology/Religion Pages 144

**Optimism** *by Helen Keller*　　　　　　　　ISBN: *1-59462-108-X*　**$15.95**
*Helen Keller was blind, deaf, and mute since 19 months old, yet famously learned how to overcome these handicaps, communicate with the world, and spread her lectures promoting optimism.  An inspiring read for everyone...* Biographies/Inspirational Pages 84

**Sara Crewe** *by Frances Burnett*　　　　　　　　ISBN: *1-59462-360-0*　**$9.45**
*In the first place, Miss Minchin lived in London. Her home was a large, dull, tall one, in a large, dull square, where all the houses were alike, and all the sparrows were alike, and where all the door-knockers made the same heavy sound...* Childrens/Classic Pages 88

**The Autobiography of Benjamin Franklin** *by Benjamin Franklin*　ISBN: *1-59462-135-7*　**$24.95**
*The Autobiography of Benjamin Franklin has probably been more extensively read than any other American historical work, and no other book of its kind has had such ups and downs of fortune. Franklin lived for many years in England, where he was agent...* Biographies/History Pages 332

| Name | |
| --- | --- |
| Email | |
| Telephone | |
| Address | |
| | |
| City, State ZIP | |

☐ **Credit Card**　　　☐ **Check / Money Order**

| Credit Card Number | |
| --- | --- |
| Expiration Date | |
| Signature | |

Please Mail to:　Book Jungle
　　　　　　　　PO Box 2226
　　　　　　　　Champaign, IL 61825
　or Fax to:　　630-214-0564

## ORDERING INFORMATION
**web**: *www.bookjungle.com*
**email**: *sales@bookjungle.com*
**fax**: *630-214-0564*
**mail**: *Book Jungle  PO Box 2226  Champaign, IL 61825*
**or PayPal** *to sales@bookjungle.com*

*Please contact us for bulk discounts*

## DIRECT-ORDER TERMS

**20% Discount if You Order
Two or More Books**
Free Domestic Shipping!
Accepted: Master Card, Visa,
Discover, American Express